# One Wonders

## *A Silas McKay Suspense*

## *Book I*

*by*

## LUANA EHRLICH

**Visit the author's website at www.luanaehrlich.com**

ISBN: 9798362658564

*To my mother, Mary Lee Pollock,*
*who delighted in sharing the book she was*
*reading with anyone who would listen.*

# List of Books
## by Luana Ehrlich

Each book can be read as a standalone novel, but for readers who prefer a series experience, the following order is suggested.

### The Titus Ray Thriller Series:

*One Step Back*, the prequel to *One Night in Tehran*

*One Night in Tehran*, Book I

*Two Days in Caracas*, Book II

*Three Weeks in Washington*, Book III

*Four Months in Cuba,* Book IV

*Five Years in Yemen*, Book V

*Two Steps Forward,* Book VI

*Three Steps Away*, Book VII

*Four Steps Missed*, Book VIII

*Five Steps Beyond*, Book IX (Coming in 2023)

### The Mylas Grey Mystery Series:

*One Day Gone*, Book I

*Two Days Taken*, Book II

*Three Days Clueless,* Book III

*Four Days Famous*, Book IV

*Five Days Lost*, Book V

### The Ben Mitchell/Titus Ray Thriller Series:

*Ben in Love,* Book I

*Ben in Charge*, Book II

*Ben in Trouble*, Book III

### The Silas McKay Suspense Series:

*One Wonders*, Book I

*Two Believe,* Book II

*Three Confess,* Book III (coming in 2023)

# PART ONE

# Chapter 1

*Monday, November 28*

I rolled the window down an inch to get some fresh air in the car, but I couldn't tell it helped all that much.

I could still smell Buck Greiner's heavy aftershave. Greiner, who had a tendency to be a little too aggressive about everything, including his personal hygiene, was in the driver's seat next to me.

At the moment, he had his telephoto lens trained on a coffee shop across from where we were parked in front of a hardware store in a strip mall in Plano, Texas, a suburb of Dallas.

He was so intent on keeping his eye on the two men inside the coffee shop, he didn't seem to notice when I lowered the window in order to dispel the pungent odor.

"Taylor hasn't given Quan anything yet. They're both just sitting there drinking their coffee and jabbering away," Greiner said. "It's gonna happen, though. I'm telling you. I know it's gonna happen."

I picked up my binoculars and trained them on the men inside. "Taylor looks worried."

"If Taylor gives Quan that flash drive, he *should* be worried."

Bruce Taylor was employed by Graham Technology Systems, a computer service company located in North Dallas. The security chief at GTS suspected Taylor of passing proprietary information to a Chinese technology company run by the Chinese government.

Liang Quan, a student at The University of Texas at Dallas, had ties to the Chinese government, and Greiner assumed Taylor was about to give Quan a flash drive containing exclusive GTS data.

In turn, he suspected Taylor was about to be the recipient of a substantial amount of cash from Quan.

It had taken Buck Greiner and his team several months to ferret out the person at GTS who was handing over the company's secrets to the Chinese government, and when Greiner called me last night to tell me they'd been able to positively identify the person as Bruce Taylor, he invited me to join him today to watch the transaction take place.

I immediately cleared my schedule to do so.

I figured Greiner had to be sure it was about to happen; otherwise, he wouldn't have asked his supervisor—that would be me, Silas McKay—to witness the handover of the flash drive to Quan.

Greiner and I worked for Discreet Corporate Security Services, where I was head of operations, and he ran the surveillance division.

DCSS was exactly what the name implied, and although Austin Tomlin, our CEO, had written a two-page mission statement for our public relations department, the first sentence in the first paragraph summarized it well enough.

*"The mission of DCSS is to provide our corporate clients with professional, discreet, and thorough investigations using interrelated systems in order to safeguard our clients' assets, people, and brands."*

Graham Technology Systems was one of DCSS's corporate clients, which was the reason Greiner and I were sitting inside a stuffy Nissan sedan in a strip mall parking lot trying to protect the assets of GTS from being compromised by one of its own employees.

"There he goes," Greiner said, using the rapid repeat mode on his expensive camera to take dozens of photographs of Taylor scooting a flash drive across the table toward Quan.

"And there's the payoff," I said, as we both watched Quan pull a manila envelope out of his backpack and hand it to Taylor.

Greiner continued taking pictures of the two men until they said goodbye to each other in the parking lot. Once they drove away, he took out his cell phone and called his backup team.

"Did you get any pictures?" he asked.

After listening a moment, he smiled. "Okay, that's perfect. Me too. I had an excellent view from here."

Seconds later, he glanced over at me and frowned. "That's right. Silas is here beside me." He shook his head. "Well, I'm not sure he'll want to do that, but I'll ask him."

After putting his phone on mute, Greiner turned to me and said, "This is Jacob Javits. He has an intern with him who's never met you, and he wants to know if the four of us could go inside and grab a cup of coffee before we head back to the office."

"Sure, why not? You know me. I never turn down a cup of coffee."

Greiner got back on the phone with Javits. "Okay. Silas is good with that. We'll meet you inside."

When he hung up, I said, "I thought I'd met all the interns back in September. Are you sure I haven't met this guy?"

"No," he said, placing his camera back in his leather camera bag, "I'm sure you haven't. This intern joined us last week, and she's not a guy. She's the daughter of the CEO of Precept Healthcare. Didn't you get the memo Personnel sent out about her?"

Precept Healthcare was another one of our corporate clients, but I fully understood why I hadn't seen the memo from Personnel.

I seldom saw an internal memo unless my administrative assistant, Claudia Hensley, decided it was worthy enough to bring it to my attention.

"No, I never saw the memo," I said. "Claudia must have thought it wasn't that important. You know how she is about my time."

He nodded. "Oh, yeah. She takes her role of gatekeeper *very* seriously." He let out a short laugh. "Are you sure she didn't work as a guard at the Huntsville prison before you hired her?"

I smiled. "No, I'm *not* sure about that. I hired her because Austin told me to hire her when I agreed to be his Director of Operations. He said I could hire my own deputy, but Claudia needed to be my administrative assistant."

Greiner motioned across the parking lot where Jacob Javits and a tall blond woman were walking toward the coffee shop. "A month ago, Personnel told me to hire Ashley Davenport as one of my interns, and since her father is Duncan Davenport, I didn't question why."

Duncan Davenport's company, Precept Healthcare, was our highest-paying client, and although I'd met with Duncan numerous times in his office suite high atop one of the dozens of skyscrapers dotting the downtown Dallas skyline, we'd never discussed his family.

As I thought about it, I couldn't recall ever seeing any family photos on display, and I usually noticed such things in order to make a connection with the client.

In Davenport's case, I didn't need to look for family photos to make a connection with him. Like me, he was a Dallas Cowboys football fan—as evidenced by an entire bookshelf full of signed photographs, autographed jerseys, a couple of footballs from their winning seasons, and even a battered helmet. Starting a conversation with him was never a problem. All I had to do was to mention the 'boys.

"I can't believe Davenport's daughter would need to work a day in her life," I said. "What's she doing interning at DCSS?"

"I asked her that same question."

"What did she say?"

"Why don't you ask her? I'd like to hear if she tells you the same thing she told me."

"Okay, we'll play that game."

◆ ◆ ◆ ◆

Cal's Coffee Café was a little different than most coffee shops, primarily because customers didn't stand in line to get their drinks.

Instead, customers were seated at tables where they were given a colorful laminated menu containing photographs of delicious-looking coffees, teas, and smoothies, which they were encouraged to study in detail before a barista appeared to take their order.

When Greiner and I walked in, Jacob Javits and Ashley Davenport were already seated at a table by the window. Both of them were looking over the extra-large menus.

The two young people presented a study in contrast. Although Javits was around thirty, he could have passed for a high school kid. His short, skinny physique, along with his baby-face looks, contributed to this misconception.

On the other hand, Ashley Davenport, who I assumed was about the same age as Javits, appeared to be much older.

I couldn't tell whether it was her stature, the tailored jacket she was wearing, or the self-assured way she held herself. Whatever it was, she definitely looked a lot more sophisticated than Javits, who was wearing a pair of worn jeans and a pullover shirt.

Greiner and I were each dressed in dark trousers, an open-collar white shirt, and a sports jacket. When we took a seat across from the young people, I was reminded of a recent conversation I'd had with my college-age daughter, Marissa, who told me her friends thought I looked like a police detective from a popular TV show.

I figured the customers in Cal's Coffee Café might think the same thing about Greiner and me, especially if they were able to tell we each had a holstered weapon underneath our jackets.

After Javits greeted me, he gestured at Ashley. "Mr. McKay, this is Ashley Davenport. She's a new intern in our Surveillance Division. Ashley, this is Silas McKay, the Director of Operations at DCSS."

Ashley immediately offered me her hand, and when I reached across the table to shake it, she said, "Mr. McKay, it's a pleasure to finally meet you. My father speaks very highly of you. He told me to be sure and make your acquaintance as soon as I got the chance."

"It's nice meeting you, Ashley. Please tell him I said hello."

"I definitely will."

"By the way, you can call me Silas." I glanced over at Javits. "I'm not sure why Jacob introduced me as Mr. McKay. We don't usually stand on formality around here."

Javits shrugged. "Uh . . . force of habit, I guess. Anyone older than me I always introduce as . . ." He paused and grimaced a little. "I'm sorry. I didn't mean to imply you're old, Silas. I was just trying to show respect for someone who's . . . uh . . ."

Greiner waved his hand at him. "Stop digging, Jacob. That hole you've already dug for yourself is deep enough as it is."

I nodded. "If I were you, Jacob, I'd quit talking altogether."

Javits smiled and picked up his menu. "I'm ordering a mocha latte. What's everyone else having?"

◆ ◆ ◆ ◆

After the barista came and took our orders, I noticed Ashley kept looking over at me like she had something on her mind.

I tried to help her out. "I usually make it a point to meet all the interns when they come to work for us, so I apologize I haven't met you sooner. Would you mind telling me a little bit about yourself?"

"Oh, not at all," she said, tucking a strand of her honey-blond hair behind her ear. "The short version is I graduated from SMU with a business degree, went on to get my master's, and after bumming around Europe with two of my sorority sisters for a few years, I came back here to Dallas, where I went to work for my dad at Precept Healthcare. But, after I spent five years sitting at a desk looking at a bunch of numbers, I told him I didn't think the corporate life was for me, and I needed to find something else to do with my life, something a lot more exciting."

She paused when the barista returned with our coffees.

Once he left, I said, "Did your father agree with your decision not to work for him?"

She took a sip of her coffee and nodded. "He agreed with my decision not to work at Precept, but he didn't agree when I told him I was thinking about applying to the Central Intelligence Agency."

I gave a short laugh. "No, I don't imagine he did. Granted, that would be a lot more exciting than a corporate job, but it would also be a lot more dangerous."

Javits waved his hand in my direction. "You need to listen to him, Ashley. Silas knows what he's talking about. He served eight years in the Defense Intelligence Agency before coming to work for DCSS."

"Yes," she said, nodding her head, "that's what my dad told me. He said you were a covert officer in clandestine operations for the Defense Department. I'd love to hear more about that sometime."

"A lot of what I did is still classified, so there's not much I can say about it."

"Oh sure, I get that."

"So your father talked you out of applying to the CIA?"

"Yeah, pretty much. He suggested I try something else instead."

Greiner asked, "Something a little less dangerous?"

"Less dangerous, but still exciting. He suggested I get my private investigator license and go to work for a PI agency. After doing some research, I decided to attend the Professional Investigators Academy at the University of North Texas."

"Good choice," I said. "We have several investigators working for us who've gone that route."

"When I finished the academy, I got my PI license, but then I realized I didn't want to go to work for someone else; I wanted to be my own boss. It took me awhile, but I finally convinced my dad to help me set up my own agency. He agreed to do that on one condition."

She glanced over at me and smiled. "Can you guess what that was?"

Greiner looked amused, as if he already knew the answer to her question. As soon as I noticed that, I figured I knew the answer too.

"Did he want you to do an internship with DCSS?"

She nodded. "Not just with DCSS. He specifically wanted me to spend time with you. He said he was sure you could teach me a lot."

I wasn't expecting that.

I took a drink of coffee to cover my surprise.

Spending time with Ashley Davenport—or any other woman for that matter—was the last thing I wanted to do.

Six months ago, I lost my wife to brain cancer.

Emma and I had been together since high school, and when she died, a part of me died with her.

Specifically, that part of me that wanted to be around another woman.

# Chapter 2

Emma and I met at a high school dance in Sherman, Texas. When we graduated, we went off to the University of Texas together, got married during our sophomore year, and were a month away from celebrating our twentieth wedding anniversary when she died.

Now, I was having difficulty even carrying on a conversation with the opposite sex. Thus, the thought of having to spend time with an independently wealthy woman, someone who wanted me to teach her the finer points of conducting an investigation so she could start her own PI agency with her daddy's money, was distasteful to me.

"So what do you say, Silas?" Ashley asked, tapping her manicured finger on the side of her cappuccino cup. "Would you mind being my mentor during my internship?"

Javits stared at her like she was out of her mind, and Greiner immediately jumped in and said, "Well, Ashley, I'm sure Silas would love to do that, but he's—"

"Sure, Ashley, I'd be happy to be your mentor," I said, cutting Greiner off in midsentence, "as long as you don't mind taking orders from me, working odd hours, watching boring surveillance videos, and following vehicles all over the Metroplex."

She smiled. "I'm good with all of that." She reached inside her handbag and pulled out a business card. "Here's my number. You can call or text me anytime."

Ashley's card turned out to be her own business card, not the kind of cheap card DCSS issued to its temporary employees.

"I see you've already chosen a name for your agency," I said. "Precept Detective Agency has a familiar ring to it."

Ashley looked slightly embarrassed. "I doubt if anyone will associate that name with Precept Healthcare, but I decided having that name was a way I could thank my dad for financing my business."

I didn't agree with her. The fact that her last name was Davenport and her PI agency was called Precept pretty well guaranteed people would connect her with her father's healthcare business.

However, none of that was any of my business.

What *was* my business was making sure Precept Healthcare remained a client of DCSS, and keeping Duncan Davenport happy by mentoring his daughter was a way I could do that.

"Our interns usually sign a contract with us for a year. Is that what you did or is your internship only temporary?"

"Oh no, it's not temporary. I signed a year's contract. It will take that long for the construction crew to finish my office building. Precept Detective Agency will occupy the first floor of a three-story office complex off the Dallas North Tollway near the Galleria."

Javits spoke up. "You should get some good paying clients from that area. What will you do with the other floors of your building?"

"The office complex actually belongs to my father. He plans to lease out the other two floors."

A few minutes later, when the barista delivered the check to our table, Ashley insisted on picking up the tab. "Let me get this," she said, handing him her credit card. "It's the least I can do after I was the one who insisted we take a coffee break so I could meet Silas."

None of us protested.

◆ ◆ ◆ ◆

After telling Ashley I'd be in touch, Greiner and I returned to his vehicle, where he began pelting me with questions.

"Are you sure you're okay with what happened in there? I mean, wouldn't it make more sense if I got one of our female investigators to work with Ashley? Or what about Conrad? He used to have his own PI agency. You know he wouldn't mind spending time with her."

"Yeah, that would make perfect sense, but do you really think passing her off to Conrad would satisfy Duncan Davenport?"

Greiner, who knew Davenport almost as well as I did, shook his head. "No, I don't imagine it would. I apologize, Silas. I had no idea she was going to put you on the spot like that. When I interviewed her, she told me her father wanted her to get some experience by interning with us, but she never mentioned your name in the interview."

"You've got to admit it was pretty clever the way she set that situation up so I couldn't say no."

As Greiner pulled into traffic on Alma Road, he shook his head and said, "You might call it clever; I call it pushy and rude."

"That too."

We were both quiet as we headed south on the expressway toward North Dallas where DCSS had its headquarters.

I figured Greiner, who tended to chew on a situation until he had thoroughly digested it, was either trying to come up with a plan to deal with Ashley, or he was trying to come up with a suggestion about how I could deal with her.

For my part, I was asking myself which one of the operations we were running would be suitable for an inexperienced intern, or more importantly, which one would mean I would have to spend the least amount of time with Ashley Davenport.

I hadn't made up my mind by the time Greiner got off the freeway on Mockingbird Lane.

Since we were getting near the DCSS office building—at Mockingbird and Preston Road—I wasn't surprised when he brought up her name again.

"I hope I'm not overstepping my bounds by telling you how you should deal with this situation with Ashley, but why don't you tell her she needs to have two or three months of assisting the surveillance teams before the two of you start working together."

"So you think I should put her off for a few months?"

After turning right on Preston Road, he said, "Yeah, why not? She's obviously inexperienced. Duncan shouldn't have a problem with that."

"But what good does putting her off do? I'm eventually going to have to take her under my wing and teach her how to fly."

Greiner didn't respond while he was parking the car in front of our headquarters building—a five-story concrete structure with a large granite monument sign near the front entrance. The sign had Discreet Corporate Security Services in raised lettering across the top, along with the company's logo—the letters DCSS inside a black shield trimmed in gold—prominently displayed in the center.

Below the logo were the words, "Founded by Austin Tomlin, 1998."

"Yeah, I'm not saying you don't have to make good on your commitment," Greiner said, as he turned off the engine, "but I just think putting it off for a while might be a good idea."

When I didn't say anything, he turned and faced me. "I figured you'd agree with me since you're still dealing with Emma's death."

I rested my head against the back of the seat. "That's true, Buck, but I have a feeling a few months won't make any difference. I'll still be dealing with it then too."

His voice softened. "Are you saying it's not getting any easier?"

I lifted my head and looked at him. "In some ways it is. At least it's not the first thing on my mind every morning, but in the evenings, if I'm not working, I find myself dwelling on it."

Greiner reached over in the back seat and grabbed his camera bag. "Well then, as long as you plan to give Ashley some instructions, it sounds like you should get together with her in the evenings."

"I was thinking the same thing. Maybe Ashley needs to work with me on the Lopez case."

He laughed. "Your evenings are about to be a lot more interesting."

"Yeah, I'm afraid so."

◆ ◆ ◆ ◆

Instead of going through the lobby, Greiner and I entered the DCSS building through a private entrance on the west side, something I usually did in order to avoid any media types in the reception area.

Whenever DCSS was involved in a high-profile case, journalists often camped out in the lobby, hoping to get a statement from either me or Tomlin. Yesterday, the CEO of Delmar Pharmaceuticals—one of our clients—was arrested for misuse of funds.

Now, I fully expected a couple of reporters from some of the local news organizations to be on the lookout for me, even though Tomlin had already issued a press release with the pertinent details.

The private entrance to the DCSS building opened up into a hallway where there was an employee elevator. Greiner and I took the elevator up to our offices on the fourth and fifth floors.

The Surveillance Division, where Greiner had his office suite, occupied half of the fourth floor. The Embezzlement Division took up the other half.

Once Greiner got off, I rode the elevator up to the fifth floor, where my offices were located.

I shared the fifth floor with Austin Tomlin, or rather, as the owner and CEO of Discreet Corporate Security Services, he occupied two-thirds of it, and I occupied the other third. My office suite was to the left as I exited the elevator, and Tomlin's suite was to the right.

The entrance to his suite was a single wooden door with no signage on the wall and no indication what was behind the door. On the other hand, the entrance to my suite was a glass door, providing anyone who got off the elevator a quick glimpse inside. In addition, the signage on my door had Director of Operations in bold black lettering.

Three nameplates were on the left side of the door with Director of Operations, Silas McKay at the top, followed by Deputy Director of Operations, Mike Norwell, and Administrative Assistant, Claudia Hensley.

Claudia looked up from her desk as I walked in.

"Hi, Silas. How did it go?" she asked. "Did you catch Bruce Taylor in the act?"

"Yes, and Buck got it all on camera. Taylor gave Quan a flash drive, and from the looks of the envelope he got from Quan, he was paid a handsome amount of cash for handing over the flash drive."

"Well, there you go. I'm sure Buck was pleased you were there to see it happen. He's worked on that case for over a year."

Claudia was a walking database of every open case at DCSS, and she could usually recall the details of most closed cases as well. If her memory failed her, she could always find the information with just a few clicks on her computer.

"Did I have any calls while I was out?"

Claudia rolled her eyes at me, something she often did if someone asked a dumb question. "Of course you had some calls. However, only two of them were important. You should return one of them ASAP, but the other one can wait awhile. You'll find both of them in your phone log."

She picked up a file folder and handed it to me. "Here's the research you asked me to do on the Biotech Trade Show. Personally, I think it's a little risky for any of our clients to participate, especially Esotrix BioOptics, but that's just my opinion."

She pushed her red-framed glasses up on her nose and added, "But my opinion is one I value very highly."

I smiled as I took the file from her. "I'll keep your opinion in mind as I read through these articles. As you know, I may have a hard time convincing the CEO at Esotrix to stay away from this one."

I took a few steps away from her desk, but then I suddenly stopped and looked back at her.

"Your hair looks shorter than it did yesterday. Did you get it cut?"

She ran her fingers through a section of her short white hair. "Yes, but I didn't get it cut yesterday; I had it done over the weekend. You just didn't notice it yesterday."

Claudia was not a beautiful woman, but she wasn't unattractive either. Although her facial features were sharp, they were softened somewhat by her pageboy style haircut, and by the neon-colored, oversized glasses she was fond of wearing.

I shook my head. "I guess I had my mind on other things yesterday."

"Of course, you did. You were thinking about Delmar Pharmaceuticals. By the way, the phone call you don't need to return until the end of the day is from a reporter with the *Dallas Morning News*. I'm sure she wants a statement from you."

I nodded. "And who do I need to call ASAP?"

"That would be Mr. Tomlin. He's already called you twice today. If you don't call him soon, he may walk across the hall and camp out here in the waiting room."

Uh-oh. That wasn't good.

# Chapter 3

My private office was at the end of the hallway directly behind Claudia's desk. The hallway to the right of her desk led to Mike Norwell's office and a small break room.

Mike was my deputy, and ordinarily, I would have stopped by and chatted with him a few minutes before heading back to my office, but I decided making the phone call to Tomlin was more important.

As in most organizations, a phone call from the boss always took precedence over anything else. This was especially true in Tomlin's case because he seldom called me.

His preference was to leave the day-to-day operations of his company to his three directors.

Besides me, the other two directors at DCSS were Bob Reid, Personnel, and Rachel Duffy, Administrative Services.

The fact that Tomlin was eager to speak with me probably meant something was bothering him about one of our cases. Either that, or a client was unhappy about something.

It didn't always mean something negative, though.

It could also mean he had a new client for us.

Adding new clients to the portfolio at DCSS was Tomlin's specialty.

In fact, he considered acquiring new clients his primary responsibility at the company he started after a distinguished twenty-five-year career in the Army.

When Lieutenant Colonel Austin Tomlin finally retired, he was the senior security advisor to the Secretary of Defense at the Pentagon.

Although Tomlin was born and raised in Marshall, Texas—located two hours east of Dallas—he and his wife, Wynona, chose to retire in Dallas, where his son and daughter lived with their families.

However, Tomlin didn't remain idle after his retirement.

Within a few months of leaving the Pentagon, he was asked to serve as an analyst on a major television news organization regarding security issues, and once he appeared on air, he started receiving phone calls from corporations wanting to hire him as a consultant to address their own security concerns.

It wasn't long before Tomlin had more job offers than he could handle, which prompted him to launch Discreet Corporate Security Services and start hiring personnel to help him.

Perhaps not surprisingly, he leaned toward employing people with a background in intelligence, who knew how to work independently, and who were good at handling a variety of personalities, as well as keeping secrets.

Today, after over twenty years as the company's CEO, he was still its chief spokesperson and the "face" of DCSS when it came to communicating with the media and our clients.

Tomlin excelled at that role.

Not only was he a charismatic personality, he also exuded authority and self-confidence.

However, he did have a few flaws.

Namely, he could be a little preachy and overbearing at times, not to mention slightly paranoid about security issues.

I was usually able to overlook the former.

It was the latter that gave me fits.

◆ ◆ ◆ ◆

After entering my office, I quickly walked over and sat down at my desk to make the call to Tomlin. Once I hit his quick dial button on my telephone console, I swiveled around and glanced at the mail Claudia had deposited on the credenza behind my desk.

It was in a file holder labeled MAIL, one of three file holders on the credenza. The other two were labeled WORRY and NOT TO WORRY.

The NOT TO WORRY holder was almost full, whereas the WORRY file was almost empty. I considered that a good sign.

The file holders were a Christmas gift from my wife, who received her degree in interior design from the University of Texas, and who was responsible for decorating my office.

When I moved into my office five years ago, Emma told me she wanted to purchase furniture for my office in muted hues of gray and beige. I had no idea what she was talking about, but when I returned from a trip to Japan a few weeks later, I was pleasantly surprised to see how comfortable the place looked when we stopped by my newly decorated office on our way home from the airport.

The wooden floor was covered with a beige rug that had a maroon border around it, which complemented my cherrywood desk and credenza. A few feet away from my desk was a seating area with a gray leather couch and two armchairs, and separating them was a rectangular chrome and glass coffee table.

On the left side of my desk was a wall with two large bookcases filled with books—most of them biographies—and mounted between the bookcases was a wide-screen television set centered over a beige cabinet containing a mini-refrigerator, as well as a safe.

Across the room, opposite the bookcases, was a set of windows overlooking a golf course. Whenever a client visited my office and commented on how lucky I was to have such an incredible view, I always figured they played golf.

As I was about to open the first piece of mail in my stack, Tomlin answered his phone.

"Hi, Austin," I said, "this is Silas. Sorry I missed your call. I was out on a surveillance job with Buck Greiner."

"Not a problem. Would you mind dropping by my office in the next fifteen minutes? I have a question for you."

"Sure, I'll be right over."

Having a question for me could mean anything from suggesting I go visit a client, wanting details about a case, or asking my opinion about something.

It seldom involved asking a question.

◆ ◆ ◆ ◆

Almost as soon as I stepped out of my suite to walk across the hall, Tomlin's door was opened by Beverly Sanger, his administrative assistant, a silver-haired lady with an optimistic attitude and a ready smile.

"Hi, Silas. He's waiting for you. Could I get you something to drink before you go inside?"

"No thanks. I'm good." I gestured at the navy blue arm sling she was wearing. "What happened to your arm?"

She shook her head. "Clumsy me. On Sunday, I tripped over my dog and dislocated my shoulder. A doctor in the ER popped it back into place, but now I have to wear this silly thing for at least a week."

"That doesn't sound like fun."

"It's not too bad, but it *does* slow down my typing just a bit."

"You know, Beverly, most people who dislocate their shoulder would forget about coming to work for a couple of days."

She laughed. "Not me. I love my job. Every day is something different, especially if Mr. Tomlin's your boss."

"I can't disagree with you about that."

I walked across the plush carpet and tapped on my boss's door a couple of times. He opened it almost immediately.

"Hi, Silas," Tomlin said, motioning me inside, "I thought I heard your voice. Come on in."

Austin Tomlin was about my height and weight—six feet and 180 pounds—but that's where the resemblance ended.

At 71, Tomlin was thirty years older than me, and he had the gray hairs and wrinkles to prove it.

On the other hand, even though I had a few crow's feet, I was still looking for my first gray hair.

Since I had coal black hair—courtesy of my Irish ancestors—I felt sure I'd be able to spot it the moment it made its appearance.

Once it did, I didn't intend to let it remain there very long.

◆ ◆ ◆ ◆

Tomlin's office was twice as big as my office. Even so, I often got claustrophobic if I was in there for more than an hour. I figured this was because he had a lot more furniture in his space than I had in mine, and there wasn't much light in the room.

Besides a massive executive desk in the center of the room, there was a visitors' area on one side—with a couch, coffee table, and several chairs—plus, on the other side of the room, there was a round conference table with six chairs.

Every inch of open wall space was covered in photos and memorabilia—mostly from Tomlin's military service days—and he also had a large American flag on display to the right of his desk with the Texas state flag on his left.

In addition, there were some legal-size file cabinets along one wall, as well as a couple of bookcases.

Although he had two sets of windows—one on the north side and one on the west side—they were covered in heavy draperies, and they were always closed.

When I asked him about why they were always closed, he said he did it for security reasons. I didn't inquire about that any further.

"Go ahead and sit down, Silas," Tomlin said, motioning me toward the seating area. "I'll join you as soon as I grab some files off my desk."

I walked across the room and sat down in an upholstered armchair with a tapestry print, and once Tomlin picked up a stack of files from one of the piles on top of his desk, he sat down in an identical chair a few feet away from me.

After opening one of the files, I was surprised to see him suddenly close it and lay the folders down on the coffee table. "Before I talk to you about this matter, Silas, I'd like to hear how you're doing these days. How are you adjusting to life without Emma? The last time we talked, you mentioned you were having some difficulty dealing with her passing."

I vividly remembered the last time we spoke, and Tomlin asked me how I was doing. When I told him I was having a hard time coping with the changes in my life, he responded by saying, "Well, Silas, then you must not be depending on God to comfort you in your hour of need."

I decided not to be as forthcoming about my feelings this time.

"Thanks for asking, Austin. I'm doing much better these days."

"Well, that's good to hear." He stared at me a moment. "I don't think I've seen you at Crossroads lately. Of course, I realize it's a big church, and you probably don't want to sit in the same pew where you and Emma sat before she got sick, but I hope your memories of being at church with her aren't keeping you away."

"Uh . . . no, those memories aren't keeping me away. I just haven't had a free Sunday lately."

He nodded and picked up his stack of files again. "I'm sure this has been hard on you, Silas, but through it all, I hope you've been able to keep in mind that God is in control, and he always knows what's best for us."

I believed that.

At least I thought I did.

However, a year ago, when a doctor entered the exam room where Emma and I were waiting to hear the results of her MRI, and I heard she had a type of brain cancer called glioblastoma, I had a hard time believing God knew what was best for me, especially when he said Emma probably didn't have more than six months to live.

It wasn't that I stopped believing in God at that moment.

I still believed.

I just couldn't communicate with him any longer.

# Chapter 4

Tomlin reached over and picked up the file folders. This time, he took out a memo from Falcon Aeronautics and handed it to me.

The logo for Falcon Aeronautics—a black falcon shaped like the letter F—was centered at the top. The falcon was holding a metal object that looked like the letter A in its beak.

Before I had a chance to read the memo, Tomlin said, "I spent all day yesterday with Richard Neal, the Chief Executive Officer at Falcon Aeronautics. I heard back from Richard this morning, and now I'm proud to announce his company is our newest client."

"Congratulations, Austin. I'm not familiar with Falcon Aeronautics, but I have to say they have a creative logo."

He smiled. "I thought the same thing."

"What exactly do they do?"

He pulled a brochure out of one of the files and handed it to me. "You can read about them here or go to their website later, but basically, they design engines for commercial orbital vehicles."

I glanced at the photograph on the front of the brochure. "So you're talking about engines for satellites?"

"That's right. The engines they design are used to launch communication and navigation satellites into orbit, and now they're trying to develop a more fuel-efficient engine to take advantage of other markets like weather and climate-monitoring satellites."

I thumbed through the brochure. "What kind of security concerns does their CEO have?"

"Richard is concerned about a certain employee involved in Falcon's alternative fuel research program. They have in-house security for theft protection and computer issues, but he wanted an outside investigative agency to look into questions about someone at their research facility. That's why Richard got in touch with me, and why he signed a contract with DCSS."

"How long have you and Richard known each other?"

He smiled. "He's an old Army buddy of mine. The two of us usually have lunch together a couple of times a year."

"When you say Richard has questions about one of his employees, what kind of questions does he have?"

"He wasn't specific about that, and, to be truthful, I didn't ask him for any details. Once I told him I would have my Director of Operations contact him and set up an operational plan to deal with his concerns, we talked about other things, like what's happening in Washington these days."

"Do you think Richard considers this an urgent matter?"

"I really couldn't tell. What he said to me was, 'I have a guy who works for me in my research division, and I've been wondering about him lately. Would you mind looking into his background for me?' "

"That's all he told you about the situation? He signed a contract with DCSS because he's been wondering about the guy?"

"That's right. You know how it is. One wonders. I often wonder about people who work for me."

◆ ◆ ◆ ◆

After Tomlin showed me the materials Richard Neal had given him about Falcon's research division, he asked me to work on Neal's case myself and not turn it over to Mike or one of my division heads.

"Would you mind giving this case your personal attention as a favor to me? Don't get me wrong. I'm not expecting you to do all the work yourself, but since Richard is an old friend of mine, I promised him I'd put my best investigator in charge of it."

"Sure, I can do that. I'll give him a call as soon as I get back to my office."

When I started to get up, Tomlin held up his hand. "Wait a second, Silas. I have one more thing."

I sat back down. "Oh, I'm sorry. I thought we were finished."

"This won't take long. You need to have everyone in your division change their password on our internal software immediately."

"Really? I wasn't aware there'd been a security breach."

"There hasn't been a security breach. At least, not yet. But I have a feeling Chinese hackers are trying to get into our databases, and I want to take preemptive action."

"Has something specific come to your attention?"

"No, but as you know, my instincts about this sort of thing are usually right."

I couldn't deny that, although I was never sure whether his instincts were prompted by an insider tip he received from one of his contacts at the Pentagon, or whether it was a case of his own paranoia.

"I'll let everyone in Operations know."

"Good. I've already informed Administration and Personnel." He paused a moment. "Speaking of Personnel, I suppose you know Duncan Davenport's daughter is doing an internship with us."

"Yes, I met Ashley earlier today. She told me her father is helping her launch her own PI business next year."

"That's what Duncan said when he asked me if she could intern with us. I told him I'd be happy to have her, but now that I've had some time to think about it, I'm suspicious of her intentions."

"Suspicious? In what way?"

"I think there's a good possibility she's only interning with us in order to get to know our investigators so she can offer them jobs with her new PI agency."

"I hate to disagree with you, Austin, but I didn't get that impression from her today. I think Ashley realizes she's inexperienced and needs some on-the-job-training before she tries to make it on her own."

"Well, I hope you're right."

I nodded. "I'm sure that's the case."

He shook his head. "Maybe so, but if you don't want to lose your best people when she starts her own company, I suggest you keep an eye on her."

As I left his office, I found myself questioning whether Tomlin could be right. Did Ashley have ulterior motives for interning with DCSS?

Was she just doing it to scout out potential investigators?

Suddenly, I realized I was being as paranoid as my boss.

If I didn't watch it, I'd soon be putting draperies over my windows.

Nope. I'd never be that bad.

◆ ◆ ◆ ◆

When I returned to my office, I immediately sat down at my desk where I logged into Personnel and pulled up Ashley Davenport's file.

Although she'd already given me the short version of her bio, I learned some interesting facts from the long version of her DCSS application form.

First, according to her graduation dates, it took her five years to get her bachelor's degree and four years to get her master's degree.

Obviously, she wasn't in a rush to get her education.

Or maybe she took it easy because she was spending all her time partying with her sorority sisters.

I also realized why I thought Ashley looked older than Javits when I saw them together at the coffee shop.

She *was* older. She was older by about six years.

In fact, she was only four years younger than me.

As I sat back in my chair and considered how I was going to handle mentoring Ashley, I happened to glance down at Tomlin's file on Falcon Aeronautics.

Maybe that was the answer.

If all Neal wanted DCSS to do was to run a thorough background check on one of his employees, then once Ashley and I met with him, I could show her how to get started with the assignment, and then she wouldn't need to check in with me but every few days.

That idea appealed to me on several levels, so I decided to call Richard Neal and introduce myself.

Evidently, he'd already entered my cell phone number in his contacts, because when he answered his phone, he said, "Mr. McKay, it's good to hear from you. I've been expecting your call."

"We're excited to have you as one of our clients, Mr. Neal, and on behalf of Discreet Corporate Security Services, I'd like to thank you for trusting us with your security needs."

"Well, like I told Austin, I'm not exactly sure what my needs are, but I'm anxious to discuss my concerns with someone who knows more about it than I do."

"Shall we make an appointment for us to have that discussion?"

"Yes. Do you want me to come by your office?"

"No, if you don't mind, I'd prefer to come to your office and see your facilities. When would be a good time for you?"

"The sooner the better. Could you come out tomorrow afternoon?"

I clicked over to a screen on my computer to have a look at my schedule. "Tomorrow afternoon works for me. What time do you want me there?"

"Let's say one o'clock. I'll tell our lobby receptionist to expect you."

"Could I suggest you only give your receptionist my name? When employees hear private investigators are meeting with the company's CEO, all kinds of rumors start floating around."

"I'm sure that's true. I'll tell our receptionist you're a friend of mine and just leave it at that."

"I'll also be bringing a colleague with me. Her name is Ashley Davenport. I hope that's okay with you."

"Oh, sure, whatever you think is best. Austin said I could trust you completely."

"Thank you, Mr. Neal. I look forward to seeing you tomorrow."

When he urged me to call him by his first name, I reciprocated by telling him to call me Silas, and then we said goodbye.

As soon as I hung up, I removed Ashley Davenport's business card from my pocket and called her number.

◆ ◆ ◆ ◆

While I waited for her to answer, I got up from my desk and walked over to stand in front of my windows.

I did it subconsciously, but a few seconds later, I realized what I was doing and smiled about it.

I often felt the need to take a walk, pace the floor, or gaze out the window when I was dealing with a difficult client.

I felt sure it kept my blood pressure down.

Of course, Ashley wasn't a difficult client.

Nevertheless, I was still feeling anxious about dealing with her.

"Hi, Ashley. This is Silas. I hope I didn't catch you at a bad time."

She chuckled a little. "No, it isn't a bad time. Would you believe I'm in the drive-thru to get some coffee?"

"Is that right?"

"If you're thinking I must be a coffee addict, you're not wrong."

"I'm pretty fond of the stuff myself. I won't keep you long, but I wanted to see if you were available tomorrow. I'll be visiting a new client, and I thought you might like to go with me on the interview."

"Oh, sure, I'm available anytime. Buck said he'd adjust my schedule to fit your needs."

"In that case, why don't you plan to come to my office around noon. I have an appointment with the CEO of Falcon Aeronautics at one o'clock. His company is located in Irving near DFW."

"Falcon Aeronautics. Got it."

"I'll see you then."

"Hold on a second, Silas. Do you have plans for this evening?"

"I'm sorry, what did you say?"

"I apologize. Did my phone cut out? I was just asking if you had plans for the evening. I thought we might grab a bite to eat together."

"I'm sorry, Ashley, but I'm tied up this evening."

"Sure, I understand. I'll see you tomorrow then."

"Right. See you tomorrow."

I breathed a sigh of relief.

◆ ◆ ◆ ◆

I wasn't lying to Ashley. I *did* have plans, but I admit if that hadn't been the case, I might have been tempted to lie to her.

I was having dinner with my daughter tonight.

Marissa was a freshman at Texas A&M University in College Station, three hours south of Dallas.

I hadn't seen her for several weeks, not even over Thanksgiving, because when I told her I had to work on the Delmar Pharmaceuticals investigation over the holidays, she decided to go skiing with some of her friends during her Thanksgiving break.

However, she drove up from College Station last night to see me.

When we talked this morning before I left for work, she told me she wanted to cook dinner for us tonight before driving back to A&M in the morning.

I didn't ask her why she decided to make the drive to Dallas for a twenty-four-hour visit with me.

I knew why.

Last year at this time, Emma received her cancer diagnosis.

Marissa and Emma were very close—more like best friends than mother and daughter—so when Emma passed away, I wasn't surprised when Marissa cried buckets of tears, but in the months that followed, there were times when I thought she was handling Emma's death far better than I was.

After we got Emma's cancer diagnosis, I also started to worry about Marissa. I wondered how her illness would affect Marissa's senior year of high school, but as it turned out, the whirlwind of activities around her graduation, and all that went into getting her ready to leave for college, ended up being a good thing.

It distracted her a lot.

It distracted both of us a lot.

Now, I was counting on Marissa distracting me this evening.

# Chapter 5

Marissa was born in Austin, Texas, two years after Emma and I were married and shortly after we both received our undergraduate degrees at the University of Texas.

Since Emma was eager to start using her interior design degree to help support us while I worked on my master's degree in international relations, it wasn't the most convenient time for us to have a baby.

But with some creative babysitting arrangements, Emma started her career, and I finished my graduate work, while we were both taking care of a newborn, who quickly turned into a toddler.

By the time Marissa turned three, I had my degree and was considering several job offers.

One was with a think tank in Maryland and another was with the State Department. But the one that took me by surprise was the one from the Department of Defense—an offer to become a covert operative in the Defense Intelligence Agency (DIA).

When I had my first interview at the DIA and heard what I would be doing—acquiring, analyzing, and investigating foreign military activity around the world—I decided I couldn't think of anything I'd rather be doing.

Plus, as one of the officers told me, the skills I acquired at the DIA could easily transition into a career in the security field if I ever decided to leave the Department of Defense.

The only drawback I saw to becoming a DIA officer in their clandestine services was being away from my family.

However, Emma and I agreed it was an exciting opportunity, one that came with a substantial paycheck, and if my absences became too difficult for either one of us to handle, I knew I could always resign.

The first six years of my career at the DIA passed quickly.

Although I had to spend days, sometimes weeks, working overseas—from Korea to Saudi Arabia to Afghanistan—when I didn't have an assignment, I could spend several uninterrupted days with Emma and Marissa at our home in Alexandria, Virginia.

Shortly after Marissa turned ten, there was a change in leadership at DIA, and a few months after that, my assignments became longer.

What used to be a few weeks turned into a few months.

After I came home from a four-month stay in Syria, where I was briefly hospitalized for a gunshot wound, Emma and I began talking about whether it was time for me to make a career change.

Emma was definitely for it, and while I agreed with her, I realized I couldn't possibly be happy with a nine-to-five desk job after the kind of work I'd been doing in intelligence.

A few months after I updated my resume and was considering joining the FBI, I got a call from Buck Greiner.

Greiner and I had met in Pakistan when we were both with the DIA, but not long after our assignment was over, he resigned from the agency to go to work for a detective agency—or at least I thought he'd gone to work for a detective agency.

When he called that day, I found out he was employed by Discreet Corporate Security Services where he headed up their Surveillance Division. After we chatted for a few minutes, he said he was calling because he thought I might be interested in moving to Dallas and working for DCSS.

He told me Austin Tomlin was looking for a Deputy Director of Operations, and he thought I'd be perfect for the position. Six months later, Emma and I signed the papers on a four-bedroom, two-story house in Frisco, a suburb north of Dallas, and I went to work for DCSS.

After I'd been with DCSS for three years, Tomlin promoted me to Director of Operations when the position became vacant after Bart Jimerson retired. Jimerson had been with DCSS for ten years, and I always suspected Tomlin urged him to take an early retirement.

◆ ◆ ◆ ◆

Now, when I pulled up in the driveway of our house on Stagecoach Drive, located in the Western Heights subdivision in Frisco, I was surprised to see a lighted Christmas tree in the living room window.

Instead of pulling in the garage and entering the house through the utility room, I parked my black Lexus in the driveway and walked around to the front of the house, where I saw Marissa waving at me from a stepladder next to the Christmas tree.

She was holding a tree ornament in her hand—a blond-haired angel dressed in a white billowing dress—the one Emma bought to put on the top of our tree the first year we were married.

"You're just in time," Marissa said, opening the front door for me. "I was about to put the angel on top of the tree."

"Oh . . . uh . . . I wasn't expecting this."

"Of course not. That's why I did it." She thrust the angel at me. "Go ahead. You do the honors."

I put my briefcase down on the floor and took the angel from her.

When I got on the stepladder and was positioning the angel on the top branch, Marissa said, "Hold it a second, Dad. I need to take a picture."

She pulled her cell phone out of her back pocket and held it up in front of her, tapping it a couple of times. "Okay. Got it."

After I got down off the ladder, I said, "You're not putting that picture up on social media, are you?"

She looked at me like I was a complete idiot. "Dad, do you really think I would do that? I know better than to put a picture of you up on the internet. I just wanted to take the picture because . . . well, you know . . . because Mom would have done it."

I nodded. "Yes, you're right. That's what Emma would have done."

We stared at each other a second before I reached out and gave her a hug. "Thanks for putting up the tree, Marissa. It looks great."

She stepped back and admired her work. "It does, doesn't it?"

Marissa was wearing her curly brown hair pulled back in a ponytail, which emphasized her high forehead and expressive hazel-colored eyes, two facial characteristics she'd inherited from Emma.

As I studied her profile, I suddenly realized she didn't look like a teenager anymore. She looked like an adult.

Or at least a young adult.

When Marissa was growing up, everyone—especially my mother—thought she favored me more than she did Emma.

These days, I was grateful for that.

◆ ◆ ◆ ◆

Marissa made lasagna for dinner. When I took my first bite and bragged about how delicious it was, I couldn't help but point out she'd cooked enough to feed a family of twelve.

"It's hard to make a small dish of lasagna, Dad. Besides, I figured you could eat the leftovers for several days. That way, you wouldn't have to figure out what to fix yourself for dinner."

"Fixing dinner for myself is something I don't do that often. I usually just stop at a restaurant before I get home, or grab a bite to eat with one of the guys from work."

"How *is* work these days?" she asked, dipping a piece of Italian bread in a saucer of olive oil and balsamic vinegar. "Have you met any interesting people lately?"

"I find most people interesting in one way or another, but if you're asking me if I've met a woman I'm interested in, the answer is no. Definitely not."

"I hear you. It's probably too early yet, but if that happens, I hope you won't hesitate to tell me. I really think I'll be okay with it."

I tried changing the subject. "What about you? Are you still dating 'ol what's his name?"

She wagged her finger at me. "I happen to know you don't forget names, Dad. You know perfectly well what his name is."

"Oh, I remember now. It's Gabe Marshall, isn't it? How is 'ol Gabe these days?"

She smiled. "He's good. Last week, the two of us decided to become official members of the church we've been attending. It's called Life Journey. I told you about it the last time I was here."

"Uh-huh. You said you liked their pastor as well as the singing."

She extended her palm toward me. "What about you? How are things at Crossroads these days?"

"I'm not really sure. I've had to miss several Sundays."

"Really? Several Sundays?" She tilted her head to one side. "Why have you had to miss several Sundays?"

"Uh . . . work, mainly just work. Work has kept me pretty busy."

She stared at me a moment.

"Are you sure it's just work?"

I looked away for a second.

"No, it's not all work. I'm not sure what it is, but being in church right now is really hard for me."

Before she had a chance to respond, I quickly added, "And no, it's not because being there reminds me of Emma."

"But if that were the reason, that would be understandable. I know I would feel strange going to Crossroads without her. Have you thought about attending a different church?"

"No, not really, and there's no reason for you to try to help me with this problem. I know you plan to become a psychiatrist, but I'd rather not be your first patient."

She gave me a smile. "Okay, I'll drop the subject."

"Why don't we talk about dessert. Did I see you made brownies?"

She nodded. "I just took them out of the oven before you got home. They're probably still warm. Do you want one or two?"

"Make it two with some ice cream on top."

She picked up our empty plates. "Two brownies á la mode coming right up. I bet you also want some coffee with that, don't you?"

"You need to ask?"

When she got to the doorway, she paused and looked back over her shoulder at me. "Have you considered the possibility you're mad at God, and that's why it's hard for you to be in church right now?"

I let out a short laugh. "No, Dr. McKay, I haven't considered that, but I *am* considering how delicious those fresh, out-of-the-oven brownies will taste, especially with some vanilla ice cream on top."

She gave me an exasperated look and left the room.

Once she did that, I thought about her question.

◆ ◆ ◆ ◆

Marissa and I spent the evening upstairs in our media room watching an old James Bond movie, although we were laughing at the corny dialogue more than following the plot.

Once we said goodnight to each other, and she went off to her bedroom, I went downstairs to my study and removed the Falcon Aeronautics file Tomlin had given me.

It was filled with several documents, but I figured the public relations brochure would provide an overview of the company, so I read it first.

However, just before opening it, I took a closer look at their company logo. That's when I realized the object the falcon was holding in its beak, which resembled the letter A, was actually an engine, and the blue orb underneath the falcon's claws, which I thought was just a throwaway design element, represented the earth.

Those details probably weren't important when it came to working with Falcon Aeronautics, but if my years in the DIA had taught me anything, it was that being aware of the subtleties of a situation was the key to seeing the big picture.

As I read through the documents describing the research methods the aeronautics company used to develop a fuel-efficient engine, I realized they hadn't concentrated on the engine itself.

Rather, they had researched different fuel blends.

The fuel-efficient engine was the big picture.

The fuel itself was the subtlety that couldn't be overlooked.

If a company had a design, a service, or a formula that was the one essential component to the success of the company, and an employee controlled that one component, then the person who had the most vested in that company often got worried about that employee.

Is that what was happening with Richard Neal?

Was he wondering about the loyalty of an employee?

I hoped not, because such an investigation could take several months, which was why I found myself wondering if I'd made a terrible mistake by inviting Ashley to be part of this investigation.

If so, I would find out tomorrow.

# PART TWO

# Chapter 6

*Tuesday, November 29*

When I arrived at DCSS headquarters a little before nine o'clock, I asked Claudia to let me know when Mike got in, and then I went straight to my office, where I brewed myself a cup of coffee from my own personal coffee machine.

Until a few months ago, my usual routine was to arrive at the office by eight-thirty, spend thirty to forty minutes having a time of meditation by reading a chapter from a devotional book or a chapter from the Bible, and then ending with a few minutes of prayer.

During Emma's illness, I spent less time reading Scripture and more time praying. Specifically, I prayed for her complete healing.

When that didn't happen, I was less inclined to read the Bible or meditate, and I found it almost impossible to pray.

The words just wouldn't come.

Whereas before, I could express my deepest feelings to God in prayer, the only thing I felt when I bowed my head these days was a feeling of emptiness.

There was absolutely nothing there.

It was a strange sensation because I always thought I had a close relationship with God and could ask him for anything. Usually, I got the answer I wanted. Although I tried not to judge other Christians, I was pretty sure I was more devoted to my faith than they were.

Now, I wasn't so sure.

Despite that, I still took a few minutes at the beginning of my day to have a time of meditation, and as I sat down on my couch with my coffee mug in hand, I opened my Bible to the book of Psalm and started reading from Psalm 22.

I hadn't read more than a few verses before I stopped and thought about the question Marissa asked me after dinner last night.

*"Have you considered the possibility you're mad at God?"*

Was that true?

Was that why I was having a hard time praying?

Was that why I couldn't concentrate on the Scriptures?

I hadn't come up with an answer before Claudia buzzed me on the intercom and told me Mike was in his office.

A few minutes later, I took my coffee, along with the file on Falcon Aeronautics, and walked down the hall to Norwell's office.

If I *was* mad at God, the last person I should be talking to was Mike Norwell. Although Norwell was a great friend, an outstanding investigator, and a man of integrity, he refused to have anything to do with Christianity.

◆ ◆ ◆ ◆

Norwell joined DCSS two years after I did. Previously, he'd been with the CIA as a computer analyst.

I became acquainted with him when one of our high-tech clients discovered they had a computer breach, and we realized it was the result of some newly updated software—the same software used by several government agencies.

After discovering some Russian hackers were behind it, I contacted the FBI, who put together a task force to look into the issue. The task force included all seventeen of the alphabet soup intelligence entities of our government, including the FBI, CIA, DIA, DSI, DHS, etc.

When we held a video conference call with the task force, I was impressed with Norwell's grasp of the situation and the way he handled himself with all the personalities on the task force, who were pushing their own agenda and were used to being in charge.

About six months later, when there was an opening at DCSS for a new cybersecurity division head, I contacted Norwell, who immediately got on a plane and flew to Dallas for an interview.

Tomlin was so impressed with him, he hired him on the spot.

Three years later, when I became Director of Operations, I recommended Norwell as my new deputy, and Tomlin agreed with my recommendation.

The only problem I had with Norwell was a minor one, and it stemmed from the fact he wasn't a very outgoing guy.

Basically, he preferred clicking keys on his computer instead of communicating with clients.

However, his expertise with computers, his past experience as a CIA analyst, and his ability to look at a problem and quickly grasp how to manage it were invaluable to me.

When I entered Norwell's office, I found him sitting at his desk, swiveling his head from one computer monitor to another like some bobble head doll.

"I still don't understand why you don't get whiplash from using three monitors at a time," I said.

He smiled and pointed over toward a corner of his office where there was a couch and several chairs. "Have a seat, Silas. I'll be with you in just a second."

Norwell's office was a little smaller than mine, and he didn't have a window. But since his bookshelves contained very few books, and there was nothing on his walls except a big-screen television set and a cubist-style painting of an old Commodore 64 computer—done in bright orange and neon blue—I didn't feel claustrophobic like I did in Tomlin's office.

After taking a seat in a leather armchair and placing my coffee mug on the short-legged table in front of me, I opened up the file on Falcon Aeronautics.

Usually, whenever Tomlin signed a new client, the first thing I did was to have Norwell use his computer wizardry to see what he could discover about the company and their personnel.

Almost inevitably, he would uncover some data the client hadn't revealed to us or even something they didn't know themselves.

Norwell walked over and sat down across from me. "Do we have a new client?" he asked, pointing at the file in my hand.

"Falcon Aeronautics," I said, handing him the brochure on the company. "The CEO is Richard Neal, and he's an old Army buddy of Tomlin's. From what Tomlin said, it sounds like Neal has some concerns about an employee in their research division."

I quickly went over the details of what Tomlin told me about the company and what I learned by reading through the documents.

"I have an appointment with Neal at one o'clock today. If you want to wait until I meet with him before you initiate a deep data dig on the company, I'm good with that."

As Norwell glanced through the pictures in the brochure, he said, "I'll probably do that. Do you have any idea about the company's security needs?"

"Not really, but since their CEO is wondering about one of the research guys, it might be a case of industrial espionage, especially since they're trying to develop a more fuel-efficient engine, and they're experimenting with different types of fuel blends."

"Yeah, that could be a possibility. He might be worried the guy is selling their research to the highest bidder."

"Exactly what I thought." I took a sip of my coffee. "But I'll let you know what the CEO says as soon as I meet with him."

"While you're gone, I'll take a look at these documents and see if I can do some preliminary research on the company."

Since Norwell wasn't much of a talker, I figured our conversation was over, but then he laid the file on the table, sat back in his chair, and gestured over at his desk.

"I just finished reading Buck Greiner's final report on his investigation for Graham Technology Systems, and he mentioned you were with him yesterday when Bruce Taylor passed the flash drive over to Quan at the coffee shop."

I wasn't sure why he was bringing up Greiner's investigation, but whenever he mentioned Greiner, my radar went on alert.

Norwell and Greiner didn't get along that well.

I suspected it was a case of two people having two completely different personalities.

Norwell was quiet, reticent, and computer-oriented, whereas Greiner was loud, mouthy, and action-oriented; not to mention Greiner thought anyone who worked for the CIA was a bit suspect.

When Norwell ran the Cybersecurity Division before he became my deputy, and all five division heads would meet to discuss a case, I could always count on Norwell and Greiner disagreeing with each other at least once in every meeting. The heads of Embezzlement, Industrial Espionage, and Employee Screening usually just kept quiet and watched it happen.

Now that Norwell was my deputy, those disagreements didn't happen as often, but they still happened.

"That's right," I said. "I was with Buck yesterday. He was pretty sure Taylor would do the handover with Quan at the coffee shop, so he invited me along to see it take place. Frankly, I'm a little surprised Buck included me in his final report for the Board of Directors at Graham Technology."

"Oh, I'm not surprised. Buck always uses your name when he wants to validate what he's done."

I shook my head. "I don't think that's the reason he mentioned me. I'm guessing he didn't want to take all the credit for discovering Taylor was the person handing their secrets over to the Chinese, and that's the reason he put my name in the report."

"Yeah, maybe so, especially since he wouldn't have solved the case if you hadn't suggested he put a tail on Bruce Taylor for a few days."

"I don't believe that's true, Mike. Buck would have gotten around to looking at Taylor eventually. I'm sure of that."

"Well, I'm not. He worked on that case for months and never got anywhere until you called his attention to Taylor." He hesitated a moment, as if he realized how harsh he sounded. "Be that as it may, I always appreciate how supportive you are of your personnel, Silas. I'm sure you've had to do the same thing for me a couple of times."

I smiled. "More like a dozen times."

He chuckled a little. "Okay, I hear you."

I glanced down at my watch. "I better get back to my office. I need to wrap things up before I head out to my appointment with Richard Neal."

"Who are you taking with you to your appointment?"

It was an official DCSS policy—meaning Tomlin himself instituted it—that client interviews at DCSS be conducted with a partner. It was one of the first things he told me when I came onboard.

"It's for your own safety, integrity, and liability," Tomlin said. "A client won't be inclined to accuse you, blame you, or take advantage of you as long as you take along a witness. I expect everyone at DCSS to have a colleague with them whenever they meet with a client."

I stood to my feet. "I'm taking our newest intern with me. This will be her first opportunity to see how we conduct an initial interview with a client."

"Would that intern be Ashley Davenport?"

"That's right."

He grinned at me.

"Why are you looking at me like that?" I asked.

He shook his head. "No reason; no reason at all."

"Have you met Ashley?"

"Oh, you bet. I was talking to Claudia in the reception area when Ashley was getting a tour of our facilities. You were out of the office on the Moberly case at the time."

"I'm assuming you know she's Duncan Davenport's daughter?"

"Oh, yeah, she mentioned who her father was after we were introduced. She's not shy, that's for sure."

"No, I wouldn't describe Ashley as shy."

Norwell's grin was back. "She seemed really disappointed she wasn't able to meet you."

I headed for the door. "Don't get any ideas, Mike. She told me her father said to be sure and make my acquaintance."

"Maybe so, but her interest in you seemed a little personal to me. She asked me several questions about you. One of them was how long you were with the Defense Intelligence Agency."

I paused after I opened the door. "What else did she ask you?"

"She wanted to know how long you'd been widowed."

# Chapter 7

Claudia escorted Ashley into my office promptly at noon, and after we greeted each other, she immediately walked over and looked out my window.

"Fantastic view. I told my architect I had to have a corner office with lots of windows. I'm not really a person who enjoys the outdoors, but I do like to be able to see the sun when I'm inside all day."

I nodded. "So do I."

As she turned away from the window, I gestured over at the seating area on the opposite side of the room. "If you'd like to have a seat, I'll brief you on what we'll be doing at Falcon Aeronautics today."

Ashley had on a black jacket over a solid red dress, along with a pair of black heels. Except for some earrings, she wasn't wearing any jewelry, and other than some red lipstick, I didn't think she was wearing any makeup—I wasn't positive about that, though.

As we walked over and sat down, I silently commended her on how she was dressed. Her clothing choices were entirely appropriate for meeting a new client.

Occasionally, when an intern showed up for work, Bob Reid, our Personnel Director, had to explain the proper dress code. However, I reminded myself she was the daughter of Duncan Davenport, so she certainly had the means to dress appropriately for any occasion.

As I opened up my iPad to give Ashley some facts about Falcon Aeronautics, I had the distinct feeling she was also observing how I was dressed.

At least, I had the feeling she was looking me over.

A few seconds later, she said, "Do you mind if I ask you a question before you get started?"

I looked up from my tablet. "No, of course not, Ashley. What's your question?"

"Do you always carry a weapon on you?"

I felt myself relax a little.

I'm not sure what question I was expecting from her, but it wasn't that one.

I nodded. "Always."

"I thought so."

I waited a beat or two, thinking she might give me a reason for her question, but when she didn't, I said, "I'm sure Director Reid told you our policy at DCSS is that all employees are allowed to carry as long as they're properly licensed. Can I assume, since you went through the PI Academy, you have your license?"

"Oh sure, I have my license. I grew up around guns. My father took my brother and me deer hunting from the time we were in our early teens."

"I didn't know your father was a deer hunter."

She shrugged. "For some reason, he doesn't talk about it much. He prefers to talk about football instead."

I smiled. "I'm well aware of that."

I glanced down at my iPad, but before I could say anything, she said, "If you want to know why I asked you that question, it's because when Jacob Javits and I were doing surveillance this past week, he said he seldom carried, so I just wanted to be sure how you felt about it." She motioned toward her handbag. "I always have my gun with me."

"I think Jacob is probably the exception. Most of our surveillance people have a weapon on them when they're on an assignment."

"That's good to know." She gestured at my iPad. "Okay, go ahead, Silas. Tell me about Falcon Aeronautics."

"Uh . . . I was just about to . . . uh."

"I'm sorry," she said, shaking her head. "That sounded bossy, didn't it? I admit I have a tendency to order people around even when I'm not in charge. I apologize for that."

"No problem. When you're running your own PI agency, you'll need to order people around."

She grimaced a little. "Yeah, but I'm not the boss yet. I promise I'll keep that in mind while I'm here."

I couldn't make up my mind about Ashley Davenport.

One moment she struck me as obnoxious and rude.

The next moment she seemed charming and pleasant.

Whatever her personality, I realized I wasn't feeling as uncomfortable around her as I thought I would be.

◆ ◆ ◆ ◆

After giving Ashley an overview of Falcon Aeronautics and describing the research they were doing on different fuel types, I sketched out the way I would be handling the interview with the company's CEO.

She listened quietly without saying a word until I wrapped things up and asked her if she had any questions.

"So just to clarify," she said, "you'll be doing the interview, and I'll be observing. Do I have that right?"

"That's correct, but if you think I'm not having you participate in the interview because you're an intern, then you've got it wrong."

"Well, yes," she said, brushing a lock of hair away from her face, "that's exactly what I was thinking."

I shook my head. "Whenever I conduct an initial interview with a client, I always ask the person who goes with me to be the silent partner, even if that person is my own deputy."

She looked puzzled. "Why?"

"Because our research shows new clients who connect with a single individual usually become repeat customers. Sometimes, they even hire us on an ongoing basis."

"And whoever conducts the interview will be that person?"

"That's right. If two people are asking questions and seeking information, it's less likely the client will make a strong connection with one of them. That doesn't mean you can't say something during the interview. By all means, join in if you think it might be helpful, or if I should ask you a direct question."

"Okay, I think I understand now."

I closed my iPad. "One more thing, and I know it may sound ridiculous, but something that shows the client we're interested in them is for us to take notes. So even if you have a photographic memory or you have perfect recall, I always ask anyone who goes with me to look as if they're taking notes during our initial interview."

She opened up her purse and pulled out her own iPad.

"I was already planning to ask you if I could take some notes. My memory is certainly not perfect."

"Okay, looks like we're all set then." I got up from my chair. "Let me just grab my briefcase, and we'll be on our way."

While I was walking over to my desk, Ashley stood up and headed toward the doorway. A few seconds later, I saw her stop by my bookshelves and take a look at some of the titles.

"Hmmm. I'm gonna take a wild guess and say you like biographies."

"That's a pretty wild guess. But yes, I like biographies. How about you?"

She looked over at me and smiled. "I prefer fiction myself."

"Really? What kind of fiction do you read?"

"Mostly historical fiction, but occasionally, I like a cozy mystery."

I nodded. "My late wife loved mysteries. I'm sure she read at least one book a week, maybe more."

As I snapped the clasps on my briefcase, I suddenly realized it was the first time I hadn't had a catch in my throat when I mentioned Emma.

I wasn't sure what to make of that.

◆ ◆ ◆ ◆

Falcon Aeronautics was located on Skyline Road about five miles north of the Dallas/Fort Worth airport.

The sprawling complex occupied a large acreage with lots of trees and consisted of three different buildings, along with their own parking lots. All the lots appeared to be almost full, including the one at the side of the two-story administration building where I parked my Lexus.

ONE WONDERS: A Silas McKay Suspense

After turning off the engine, I looked over at Ashley. "What can you tell me about this company just by observing their parking lots?"

She seemed surprised by my question "Ah . . . okay, let's see. Well, I guess they must be operating at full capacity since I don't see many empty parking spaces."

I nodded. "Right. Anything else?"

She looked around for a second. "There's no reserved parking for management, so I'd say the CEO wants every worker here to feel as if they're being treated the same as an executive."

"Good call. Anything else?"

"I noticed they didn't have a gated entrance. Anyone can drive onto their property." She took another look around. "I think that's it."

I pointed up at the light poles around the parking lot. "What about their security cameras?"

"Oh, I didn't notice those." She shook her head. "Obviously, I need to improve my observation skills."

From the moment I met Ashley, I questioned whether she would be willing to take instruction from me. Now, her self-deprecating statement seemed to confirm she had a teachable spirit.

"Don't beat yourself up, Ashley," I said, unstrapping my seatbelt. "Your other observations were on target. Here's why I asked you the question: Even though Richard Neal didn't hire DCSS to do an analysis of his present security setup, there's always a possibility he could ask us if we noticed anything that needed improving at his facility."

"So you always go into a situation anticipating that question?"

"Yes, when I visit a client for the first time, I'm prepared to suggest at least one way they could tighten up their security. You might be surprised at how often I get a call the next day asking DCSS to run a full security analysis of their procedures, even though that wasn't the reason they contacted DCSS in the first place."

She looked thoughtful for a moment. "That makes sense, but would that also work at my PI agency? I mean, if you were running the agency, and someone hired you, or even one of our other private detectives, what other services would you offer them?"

I shrugged. "I'm not sure. I really haven't given much thought to running a PI agency."

"Well," she said, giving me a smile, "maybe I've given you something to think about."

I considered her comment rhetorical and didn't respond.

However, I wasn't sure she meant for it to be a rhetorical comment. That bothered me a little.

◆ ◆ ◆ ◆

The lobby of Falcon Aeronautics was impressive. It was all chrome and glass and looked as shiny as a new car sitting in the showroom.

As we walked across the ceramic tile floor to the receptionist desk, Ashley's heels made a light tapping noise, which seemed to embarrass her, or maybe she was amused by it. It was hard to tell.

I decided not to comment on it.

"May I help you?" the receptionist asked.

"I'm Silas McKay and this is Ashley Davenport. I believe Richard Neal is expecting us."

"Yes," she said, taking a quick look at her computer, "Mr. Neal's assistant just messaged me she's on her way down to the lobby now."

As we waited for Neal's assistant, I took the opportunity to study the massive collage of artwork on the walls. The sight was impressive.

It consisted of gigantic photographs of different satellites hovering over planet Earth, and underneath each photograph was a nameplate which noted the satellite had reached its designated orbit because a Falcon engine had delivered a flawless performance.

Ashley and I were admiring an incredible view of our planet—one where the North American continent could be clearly seen—when a redheaded woman in a green dress approached us.

"Hi, my name's Margaret Frederick, Mr. Neal's assistant."

Ashley and I introduced ourselves, and then we followed her over to a set of elevators where we rode up to the second floor with her.

Once we arrived, Margaret indicated Mr. Neal's office was at the end of a long hallway, and as we headed down there, she lowered her voice and said, "Mr. Neal told me you're with Discreet Corporate Security Services, but he told me not to mention it to anyone else. I assure you I won't say a word to anyone."

"We appreciate that, Margaret. It makes our job a lot easier."

"I'm not speaking behind his back, Mr. McKay. In fact, I've discussed this with Mr. Neal before, but I really believe access to our property should be monitored more stringently. Do you suppose you could make that part of your recommendation to him?"

I was happy to hear Neal hadn't given Margaret the full story of why he'd engaged our services, but I was also a little ticked at him for letting her know we were with DCSS in the first place.

Ashley said, "Do you have some ideas about how the property should be monitored?"

Margaret nodded as we approached the end of the hallway. "I think we should have a gated entrance, and the property should have fencing around it. That way, if a former employee tried to get on the property, it wouldn't be that easy, and it might even make him or her have second thoughts about showing up here and shooting everyone."

When Margaret ushered us into Neal's outer office, I realized I hadn't considered the possibility he was concerned about a disgruntled worker becoming unhinged and physically endangering the lives of his other employees.

Since it was a little unusual for me not to consider all the possible scenarios of why a client wanted to engage our services, I wondered why I hadn't done so.

Had I gotten distracted?

Yeah, probably.

And the distraction was standing right beside me.

# Chapter 8

Much like the rest of the building, Richard Neal's outer office, where Margaret had her desk, was furnished in a modern contemporary style with large photographs on the wall.

That wasn't true in Neal's private office where he had more windows than wall space, a feature I really liked.

As soon as Margaret opened his door, Neal got up from his desk and walked across the room to greet us.

"Hi, I'm Richard Neal. You must be Silas McKay."

"Nice to meet you, Richard," I said, shaking his hand. "This is my colleague, Ashley Davenport."

As he shook Ashley's hand, he said, "Thank you for coming to see me on such short notice." He pointed to the two white leather guest chairs directly in front of his desk. "Please have a seat, and I'll tell you what's on my mind."

Before Neal sat down at his desk—a thick slab of black plastic supported by shiny metal legs—he gestured at a stainless steel carafe on a credenza behind him. "Could I offer you a cup of coffee or perhaps some bottled water?"

We both declined his offer.

He sat down in a two-toned leather office chair—an ergonomically designed masterpiece—and folded his hands in front of him.

"I'm not sure where I should begin. Should I tell you what prompted me to call Austin about my concerns? Or would you rather have a tour of our facilities first and then hear my story?"

"My preference would be for you to tell me about your concerns first," I said, "and then after that, you could give us a tour of your facilities. That is, as long as that's agreeable with you."

He nodded. "Copy that. Let's begin there."

Neal had short dark hair, a slightly crooked nose, and broad shoulders. It was difficult to tell how old he was, but I figured he was in his late fifties, maybe early sixties. If Tomlin hadn't told me Neal was former military, I might have guessed it by his perfect posture and his clipped way of speaking.

I leaned over, unsnapped my briefcase, and removed my iPad. A few seconds later, Ashley did the same. "If you don't mind, Richard, Ms. Davenport and I will be taking notes during our discussion. After you're finished describing the situation, we'll probably have a few questions for you."

"I'm not sure you'll need to take notes. My story doesn't have that many details in it. Basically, it's just a case of my gut telling me something's going on with one of my employees. Since this employee is an integral part of my research division, I thought it was important to find out exactly what he's up to."

"Oh, definitely. I'm sure anyone in your position would feel the same. Why don't you start off by giving us the employee's name, and then go ahead and tell us what concerns you about him."

"His name is Victor Perry, and he's the head of fuel research for our new Falcon engine. He's the brains behind our development of a new fuel blend to make our engines more efficient and thus more competitive in today's marketplace."

"Would you mind spelling that name for us?" I asked.

As he did so, I typed it into my notes, and Ashley did the same, or at least she appeared to be taking notes.

Once I looked up from my tablet, Neal continued, "In order to tell you what concerns me about Perry, you probably need to know that the competition to produce rocket propulsion engines like we build here at Falcon is increasing every day. There are so many new industries out there using small satellites to expand their capabilities that several of the large rocket engine manufacturers have now decided to develop their own version of a satellite propulsion system."

"Can I assume that means they're developing their own fuel blends as well?" I asked.

"Correct. With that background, you can understand why I'm concerned about keeping Falcon's own proprietary fuel blend a secret, as well as guarding the enhancements we've made to our engines to make them more fuel-efficient."

"Yes, of course. That makes perfect sense."

Ashley chimed in. "Oh, absolutely."

Neal looked over at her and nodded. "I've recently increased our in-house security in all three of our buildings. Besides adding security personnel and video monitoring, I've installed a check-in/check-out system for all the small mechanical components. That way, they can't leave the area in an employee's briefcase or lunch bag."

"What about your cybersecurity system?" I asked.

"I'm not a big computer person myself, but I pay our computer experts big bucks to keep an eye on that for me."

"Yet despite all these precautions, you're still worried about the integrity of someone who heads up your fuel research division?"

"Well, that's just it. I don't know whether to be worried about Victor or not. I'm just wondering about him. Let me show you a picture, and then I'll tell you why I suddenly got concerned."

Neal picked up his cell phone and quickly scrolled through some screens. Once he found what he wanted, he turned the phone around so we could see it.

Ashley and I both leaned forward to look at it.

It was a photograph of two men sitting in a parked car. I figured it was parked, because the man behind the wheel—a blond-haired man with a sharp chin and a longish nose—was turned sideways, gesturing at the man in the passenger seat next to him.

The passenger had dark brown hair, bushy eyebrows, and thin lips. He was staring over at the driver, but it was impossible to tell what he was thinking. He had absolutely no expression on his face.

"The man behind the wheel in this picture is Victor Perry. I have no idea who the other man is."

Neal turned his phone around and sat back in his chair.

"That's what I want you to find out. Who is that man?"

◆ ◆ ◆ ◆

Before I could ask Neal where and under what circumstances the picture was taken, he proceeded to give me all the details.

"As I was leaving work about two weeks ago, my wife called and asked me to pick up a few things for dinner. Since there's a Homefront Grocery Store a couple of blocks from here, I pulled in there, and as I was about to get out of my car and go inside, I noticed a red pickup in the next row over from where I was parked. That's when I took this picture. Victor was sitting in the pickup—it's his personal vehicle—and it was obvious he and the other man inside were engaged in an intense conversation."

Neal raised his hands in the air as if to prevent us from saying anything—although I had no intention of interrupting him. "I know what you're thinking: The fact that I saw Victor having a conversation with someone in a parking lot doesn't necessarily mean he was giving away Falcon's secrets. I understand that. However, when I came out of the store twenty minutes later, they were still talking."

He paused as if he thought one of us might make a comment, but since I'd already told Ashley not to rush a client when he or she was explaining the problem, I followed my own advice and kept quiet.

"The whole situation seemed really odd to me. I realize people meet in parking lots when they're selling concert tickets or buying stuff from individual sellers, but I didn't think that was what was happening here. The two men were just talking. There was no money or merchandise being exchanged. Finally, the other man got out of Victor's car and went over and got in a Chevy Suburban and drove off. I took a picture of his car, but I didn't get his license plate."

He flipped through his mobile phone to the next picture and showed it to us.

Once we glanced down at it, he shrugged and said, "Well, that's my story. I want to know who the man in this picture is, and why he and Victor were meeting in a grocery store parking lot. I want to know if Victor is engaged in industrial espionage, and I want to know if he's selling Falcon's secrets to the highest bidder. As the CEO of Falcon Aeronautics, I feel I have the right to have him investigated."

"I understand why this concerns you," I said. "I'm sure I'd feel the same way."

"I tried to do a little snooping on my own by following Victor when he left work the next day, but once I realized he was on his way home, I gave that up. I also tried to follow him the next day, but when I pulled up behind him at a red light, and he waved to me, I decided I was no good at this, and it was time to call a professional. That's when I got in touch with Austin."

"What about your own security people? Did you ask them to keep an eye on Victor for you?"

"No, this is much too sensitive for our in-house people. I don't believe they're capable of handling something like this."

I stroked his ego a little. "That was very wise on your part."

He smiled and gestured at his phone. "Shall I send these photographs to your cell phone?"

"Yes, please do."

While he was texting the pictures to me, he said, "I'm sure you must have some questions for me about this, so fire away."

I nodded. "My first question is, how likely is it that Victor could be looking for another position? Is there any possibility he was meeting someone to discuss a job opening?"

"That thought *did* cross my mind, but if he's considering going to work for another company, I figured he wouldn't be meeting his future employer in a parking lot."

"I tend to agree with you, but we'll look into that possibility as well. We'll need Victor's biographical information, a good photograph of him and his family, and I'd like to have access to his email account here at work. If he has a company cell phone, we'll need your permission to see those records also."

"He doesn't have a company phone. My assistant has a couple of flash drives with Victor's personnel information on it, but I'll make sure she adds some photographs and his email account to those."

"I can't think of any other questions I have for you." I looked over at Ashley. "Do you have any questions for Richard?"

She nodded. "Have you spoken with Victor since you saw him in the parking lot at the grocery store?"

He chuckled a little. "Well, yes, as a matter of fact, I have. Last week, after a meeting with my research people, I asked Victor to stay behind and give me an update on XLM-15. That's the name of the most promising fuel for our new engine, the Ventura. I wanted an update from him, but I also wanted to gauge his state of mind."

"And what was your conclusion?" I asked.

He shrugged. "He seemed perfectly normal. He wasn't nervous around me or anything like that."

"Did you ask him any personal questions?"

"No. There's never any need to ask Victor any personal questions. Whenever he's talking to you, he's usually talking about himself or how brilliant his kids are."

"Is he married? Divorced? How many kids does he have?"

"He has two kids. I think he's married, but he doesn't talk about his wife that much, only his kids, who are both students at MIT."

"Are you saying he's a little narcissistic?" Ashley asked.

"More than a little. However, Victor is such a brilliant man in his particular field, I'm willing to overlook it. What I'm not willing to overlook is betrayal."

I made a quick note on my iPad, and then I looked over at Ashley. "Do you have any other questions for Richard?"

She closed her tablet. "No, I don't believe I do."

"Well then," Richard said, getting up from his desk, "I guess you're ready to have a tour of our facilities now."

I shook my head and picked up my briefcase. "No, Richard, unless you have some objection, I've changed my mind about that. After what you've just told me, I'm reluctant to meet Victor in person, or for that matter, to be seen getting a tour of your operations."

He looked puzzled. "Okay, that's not a problem, but what made you change your mind?"

"Austin wants me to be personally involved in your case, so along with the members of a surveillance team, I'll probably be shadowing Victor myself. If I were to meet him today, and then he happened to spot me in a parked car a few days later or noticed me following him on foot, there's a possibility he might recognize me."

"Sure, that makes sense."

ONE WONDERS: A Silas McKay Suspense

"When I get back to the office, I'll work up what we call our Strategic Action Scheme. Sometimes, you may hear us refer to it as the SAS, but it's basically our plan for how we'll be working your case. Once we do that, I'll be contacting you to let you know how we plan to proceed with getting you the answers you need."

"Strategic Action Scheme. Did Austin come up with that name? That kind of terminology sounds exactly like him."

I smiled. "He probably did, but it was already being used when I got to DCSS. That's one of the perks of being the CEO; you get to name things."

Ashley gestured at an arrangement of mockups—scaled-down versions of Falcon engines—displayed on the credenza behind Neal. "I bet you named all of your designs, didn't you, Richard?"

He looked pleased at her observation. "Yes, I did."

He turned around in his chair and picked up the largest one. "This is my favorite. I named it Serenity."

He gave us a brief rundown on why he named it Serenity.

I didn't pay much attention to him.

I was too busy watching Ashley pretending to be interested in Neal's commentary. She'd obviously homed in on something he was eager to talk about, and I was chastising myself for not noticing the display of mockups and commenting on them myself.

I decided there wouldn't be any need for me to give Ashley lessons on schmoozing people in order to make a connection with them.

She'd already learned that lesson herself, and from what I could tell, she was very good at it.

I also decided I would do well to keep her abilities in mind as we worked together on Victor Perry's case in the coming days.

I had a feeling she wasn't above schmoozing me as well.

# Chapter 9

On our way back to DCSS headquarters from our meeting with Richard Neal, I waited to see what Ashley would say about our visit before bringing it up myself.

I didn't have to wait long.

We were barely on the freeway before she started asking me questions. "How do you feel about Richard's gut instinct that something is going on with Victor Perry? If you were him, would just seeing an employee talking to someone in a parked car merit a full-blown investigation?"

"If *my* company's future was dependent on developing new technologies in order to stay one step ahead of the competition, I'm pretty sure I'd be wary of anything that seemed a little unusual with my top researcher. So, yes, I'd say it bears investigating."

She was quiet for a few seconds.

Finally, she nodded and said, "I'm sure you're right. Industrial espionage is a very serious business."

"But that doesn't mean you shouldn't be skeptical of what triggered his reason for hiring us. It's always better to keep an open mind about an investigation until all the facts are pointing in one direction, even if the client has already made up their mind about it."

"And I suppose if this doesn't turn out to be a case of Victor Perry selling Falcon's secrets, then our investigation of him will at least put Richard's mind at ease and stop him from wondering about Perry."

I nodded. "That would be a good outcome, all right."

She adjusted her seatbelt so she could face me. "I'm not looking for compliments, Silas, but do you mind telling me how I handled myself with Richard? Were my comments appropriate? Do you think he made a connection with you?"

I looked over at her and smiled. "Whether Richard made a connection with me is something that remains to be seen, but I have no complaints about how you conducted yourself today, Ashley. In fact, I thought your question about whether Richard had spoken with Victor since the incident in the parking lot was a good one."

"Really? Why?"

"Because his answer gave us some additional insight into Victor. Now we know the man has narcissistic tendencies."

She chuckled a little. "Oh, good. After that question popped out of my mouth, I wasn't sure I should have asked it."

"It worked out fine. You can bet that kind of information won't show up on Victor Perry's curriculum vitae."

"So what happens next? Where do we go from here?"

"Next, we put together the Strategic Action Scheme. Nothing happens at DCSS until we get that done."

"How do you go about putting it together? Do you do it yourself, or is it a joint effort with the division heads?"

"The SAS is a collaborative effort with the DCSS division heads. If everyone's available, I'll schedule it for tomorrow morning."

I hesitated for a moment, but then I added, "You can sit in on the meeting if you like. I'm sure other interns will be there as well."

"Thank you. I'd love to do that. I'll put it on my calendar."

She pulled out her phone. "Will the meeting be in your office or in one of the conference rooms?"

"I'll have Claudia schedule it for eleven o'clock in the third-floor conference room, and I'll have her text you and confirm that time."

"Okay, got it."

As she put her phone away, my own phone started vibrating.

I slipped it out of my pocket and took a quick look at the screen.

It was Marissa.

"I'm sorry, but I really need to take this call."

"Sure, no problem." She smiled. "I'll watch the road for you."

"Hi honey. Is everything okay?"

"Yes, everything's fine. I just wanted to let you know I'm back at College Station now."

"How was the trip?"

"I didn't run out of gas or have a flat tire, so all's well."

"Thanks for letting me know, Marissa. I really enjoyed having dinner with you last night."

"Me too, Dad. We'll talk in a few days, okay?"

"I'll look forward to it."

After I hung up, I had to concentrate on getting off the freeway, and it wasn't until I turned on Mockingbird Lane that I realized Ashley hadn't said a word since I took the call from Marissa.

As I reviewed what she must have overheard, it occurred to me she probably thought she was listening to a conversation between me and my dinner date from last night.

For some reason, I decided to dispel that notion.

"That was my daughter, Marissa."

"I see."

"She's a freshman at Texas A&M. She came home for a couple of days this week, and last night she insisted on making dinner for us. She always calls to let me know she made it back to school safe and sound."

She nodded. "I used to do the same thing for my dad. I know he worried about me until he got that phone call."

I wasn't sure what to make of her statement.

Did she see me as a father figure?

◆ ◆ ◆ ◆

After we entered the DCSS building, I handed Ashley one of the flash drives Margaret had given us after we left Neal's office. It contained Victor Perry's biographical information, as well as other personnel information, and I assigned her the task of reviewing the material.

"Once you've done that," I said, "I'd like for you to write up a summary of the key points. Then let's plan to meet in my office at nine o'clock tomorrow to go over what you found."

After taking the flash drive from me, she held it up in front of her for a few seconds. "I want you to know, Silas, I really do appreciate the opportunity to work with you on this. I know watching you put together a case from the very beginning, as well as being able to assist you with it, will be a valuable learning experience for me."

She reached over and laid her hand lightly on my arm. "I really can't thank you enough for being willing to mentor me like this."

Before I could say anything, the elevator doors opened on the fourth floor, and she stepped off, giving me a brief wave before she headed down the hallway to her office.

After punching the button for the fifth floor, I leaned up against the side of the elevator and closed my eyes.

Suddenly, I felt extremely tired, like all the energy had been sucked out of me. I couldn't specifically identify what had caused me to feel depleted all of a sudden, but during the last six months I'd had several similar experiences.

It usually happened when I found myself in a situation that brought back memories of all the good times Emma and I had shared together—like eating at a favorite restaurant, watching an old movie, or attending a Dallas Cowboys football game.

This time, though, I couldn't pinpoint why I felt so fatigued.

◆ ◆ ◆ ◆

Immersing myself in a case, along with having some caffeine, was usually a good way for me to reenergize, so once I got to my office, I made myself a cup of coffee and got to work on the Victor Perry case.

Broadly speaking, a Strategic Action Scheme defined the scope of the investigation, outlined how to obtain the relevant information to run it, and assigned personnel to do the work.

Putting together the SAS was a collaborative effort with my division heads, who were encouraged to weigh in on how to approach the client's security problem. Sometimes, the process got a little messy, but in the end, the result was a comprehensive plan of action.

As I went over my notes from our meeting with Neal, I realized in the Victor Perry case, we would be investigating two different things.

Not only did Neal want to know if Perry was selling trade secrets, he also wanted us to identify the man speaking to Perry in the parked car. Although the two appeared to be connected, how we went about obtaining the answers involved different approaches.

I pulled out my cell phone and looked at the picture Neal had taken in the parking lot. Then I immediately got Mike Norwell on my office intercom.

"Hi, Mike. I just got back from Falcon Aeronautics, and I was wondering if you were free to talk about the case now."

"Sure thing. Shall I come down to your office?"

"No, I'll come and see you in a few minutes. Right now, I'm sending you a couple of photographs. I'll tell you about them when I get there."

On my way down to Norwell's office, I stopped off at Claudia's desk and gave her all the pertinent information to open up a case file on Victor Perry. Once she made it official and entered it into our database, she informed me the file name was now VP-489.

"Shall I also set up the SAS meeting?" she asked.

"Yes. See if you can schedule it with our division heads for eleven o'clock tomorrow morning. I've invited Ashley Davenport to be present, so confirm that time with her too."

"I know Tyler Hudson flew up to Oklahoma City to run down a lead on the Kohler case, so I doubt if he'll be able to make it."

Hudson was the head of the Embezzlement Division at DCSS, so I told her to notify him of the meeting, but to assure him he wouldn't need to fly back, since he wouldn't be needed on VP-489.

"If you don't need Tyler on this case," Claudia said, "I suppose that means no one at Falcon is stealing from the company,"

"Well, they may be stealing, but they're not stealing money."

"In that case, I'll make sure Grant Edman is at the meeting."

Edman was the head of our Industrial Espionage Division, and after I agreed he needed to be there, I said, "I gave Ashley some documents to review, and once I hear back from her, I'll have a document package ready for you to print up before tomorrow's meeting."

She pushed her glasses up on her nose. "And how did Ms. Ashley Davenport conduct herself at the meeting with Mr. Neal? Did she monopolize his time by asking him a dozen questions?"

I wasn't exactly sure what was behind Claudia's sarcastic tone, but I suspected it was a combination of a couple of things.

First, Claudia instantly disliked anyone who used a position of privilege to take advantage of someone, and second, she possessed an almost fanatical desire to protect me from having to deal with inconsequential matters.

Thus, I imagined she viewed Ashley Davenport as someone who was taking advantage of me because her father was an important DCSS client. Since I didn't doubt for a minute she knew Ashley had plans to start her own PI agency, perhaps she also thought she was using me for her own ends—Claudia made it her job to know anything there was to know about anyone at DCSS.

"No, Ashley didn't ask Richard a dozen questions; it was more like a couple. And her conduct with him was entirely appropriate. Is there some reason you thought she might bombard him with questions?"

She waved her hand dismissively. "I was just going by my own experience with her. She certainly asked me a lot of questions."

I smiled. "I'm sure someone told her you were the go-to person around here when it comes to information, and she wanted to take advantage of your expertise."

"That may be true, but personally, I think she's here to take advantage of you because someone told her you're Mr. Nice Guy."

"You could probably dissuade her of that notion."

She gave me a mischievous grin. "Oh yeah, I have some stories I could tell her, all right."

◆ ◆ ◆ ◆

When I entered his office, Norwell immediately motioned me over to his desk and pointed at one of his monitors.

"Can you guess what I'm looking at here?" he asked.

I studied his screen for a few seconds.

"It appears to be a bunch of people working at their desks in an office building, and it's obvious management believes in the open office concept. Everyone looks pretty busy, except for that couple over there in the corner."

"Correct, but do you know what company this is?"

"Hmmm. Is it Falcon Aeronautics?"

He looked surprised. "Is that a lucky guess?"

"No. I recognize the photographs on the wall. I noticed identical ones hanging in the lobby of the administration building. How did you get this video? Don't tell me you've hacked into their system already."

"I'm afraid so." He shook his head. "Their computer security system is totally inadequate."

"Well, their CEO isn't worried about their computer security system as much as he's concerned about one person, namely, his Director of Fuel Research, Victor Perry. In that photograph I just sent you, Perry is the person sitting in the driver's seat."

"Who's the other man?"

"Richard has no idea, but he wants us to identify him ASAP. For the moment, we'll have to tag him as the Unknown."

Norwell pulled up the photo and studied it while I was going over the details of my meeting with Richard Neal.

After I told him I'd scheduled the SAS meeting for tomorrow morning, he said, "If it's okay with you, I'll run the Unknown's photograph through my facial recognition software before our meeting tomorrow."

"I was just about to ask you to do that. When we go into our SAS meeting, if we've identified the Unknown, half our work on the case will already be done."

He nodded. "I probably won't know anything about the guy until in the morning, but if I happen to get a positive ID on him sooner than that, I'll let you know."

"Sounds good."

He gestured at the monitor. "What about Falcon's computer security issues?"

"I don't suppose I could talk you into working up a presentation to sell Neal on the idea of allowing DCSS to run things for him, could I? You'd get plenty of kudos from Tomlin if you did that."

He grimaced. "I'll be glad to work up the presentation as long as someone else does the presenting. Tomlin might even want to do it himself."

"You're probably right. It's obvious he and Richard Neal know each other pretty well. When Ashley and I met with Neal today, he mentioned Tomlin several times."

"Speaking of Ashley," Norwell said with a smile, "how did you feel about working with her today? Was it a problem for you? Were you uncomfortable around her?"

A few months ago, during a particularly bad time, I shared with Norwell how uncomfortable I felt around women, and how difficult it was for me to carry on a conversation with them.

His advice for me was to get a dog.

He told me when he went away to college he was having similar issues relating to women, but when he got a dog, female relationships became a lot easier for him.

Whenever Norwell gave me off-the-wall advice about personal issues—which he often did—my usual response was to tell him I would take his advice under consideration.

That's what I did.

I considered it for all of two seconds.

"No," I said, "I didn't feel as uneasy around Ashley today as I expected I would, but she's very comfortable in her own skin, so that probably helped a lot."

"I still think you need a dog."

I shook my head. "I don't have time to go out looking for a dog right now. I'm too busy looking out for our clients."

"Don't worry about that. If there's a dog in your future, he'll probably find you. That's what usually happens. Your busy life won't matter to him."

"I didn't know that."

Fortunately, I didn't believe there was a dog in my future.

Of course, I'd been wrong about my future before.

Very wrong.

# PART THREE

## Chapter 10

*Wednesday, November 30*

On my way into work, I got a text from Mike Norwell asking me to stop by his office as soon as I arrived at DCSS headquarters.

I figured that meant he had some information about the Unknown in the Victor Perry case. When I stopped at a red light, I sent him a text.

*"Is this about the Unknown?"*

*"Right. I found him."*

*"My ETA is ten minutes."*

Although I arrived in the parking lot in ten minutes, I stopped off at my office and brewed myself a quick cup of coffee before I knocked on Norwell's door.

When he told me to come in, he was putting a coffee pod in his own coffeemaker. Pointing at my cup, he asked, "Is that a fresh cup or would you like a refill?"

"I just made it. That's why I'm five minutes late."

I started to sit down on the couch, but he quickly waved me off and said, "Don't sit down just yet. Come on over to my desk, and I'll introduce you to our Unknown."

"How long did it take you to find him?"

"The software did all the heavy lifting, of course, but when I got here at eight, the timestamp showed a positive ID around two o'clock this morning."

He gestured at the monitor on the left side of his desk where the Unknown's face was displayed. However, this time, I wasn't looking at the photograph Neal had taken of him in the parked car.

This time, I was looking at the type of photograph taken when a suspect was booked into jail.

I was looking at his mug shot.

Beneath the photo was the name Devin Snead, a booking number, and the location where the booking took place, the Dallas County Sheriff's Department.

"So our Unknown is a criminal," I said. "Did you find out why Devin Snead was booked into the Dallas County jail?"

He smiled as he sat down at his desk. "What do you think?"

I grinned at him. "I think you're a very resourceful person who knows how to find out stuff. So what did Snead do?"

"He was arrested for receiving stolen property."

He swiveled one of his monitors around so I could see it. "You can read the charge for yourself."

I sat down in the guest chair at the side of Norwell's desk and read about Devin Snead's arrest. I admit I was surprised to learn he owned Goldie's Pawn Shop on Kimble Avenue in South Dallas, one of the rougher parts of the city.

The article indicated Snead was arrested for purchasing a cache of weapons from an individual who claimed they were part of an estate sale. However, in reality, the guns had been stolen from a gun store two days earlier. Thus, Snead was charged with knowingly receiving stolen property. There was nothing in the article about how Snead knew the guns were stolen.

The next article on the screen was dated a few months later and noted Snead was found guilty of a misdemeanor charge and sentenced to eight months in jail.

I shook my head. "I don't know what to make of this, Mike. Why would Victor Perry be meeting with someone like Devin Snead?"

"You got me, but now that we have a name, I'll be able to do some more digging on him." He took a sip of his coffee. "Hopefully, I'll have some answers for you before our SAS meeting."

I glanced down at my watch. "You've still got a couple of hours."

"The background check I ran on Victor Perry also turned up a few things, but those can wait until our meeting."

"Something about him selling Falcon's trade secrets?"

"No, nothing like that. It's mostly personal stuff."

I grabbed my coffee and headed for the door. "I'm having Ashley go through the personnel information Richard gave us on Perry, so we'll see what she discovers."

He looked a little surprised. "I'm assuming you'll be going through the same information just to make sure she doesn't miss anything."

"Yeah, but I didn't tell her that."

◆ ◆ ◆ ◆

When I got back to my office, I realized I didn't have time for my daily Bible reading before Ashley arrived, but I did pause a few minutes and say a prayer for Marissa.

Even though I had a hard time praying for myself, I never had a problem asking God to watch over her. I also mentioned 'ol what's-his-name, Gabe the boyfriend, and their relationship.

After I finished, I put together an agenda for the SAS meeting, along with some pertinent information about Victor Perry, but at the last minute, I decided to wait and see what Ashley had to say about Perry before having Claudia prepare copies for everyone.

Ashley knocked on my door a few minutes before nine o'clock.

Since Claudia hadn't buzzed me to let me know Ashley was here, I was surprised to see her when I opened the door.

"Oh, hi, Ashley. Come on in."

"Claudia was on the phone, so I decided I could announce myself. I suppose that's okay, isn't it?"

"Oh, sure. Fine with me."

It was fine with me, but I wasn't so sure about Claudia.

I had no doubt I'd hear about it if it wasn't fine with her.

I asked Ashley to have a seat in one of the chairs in front of my desk, and once she sat down, she removed some papers from her purse.

"I printed out my notes on what I learned about Victor. Do you want to look them over, or shall I just tell you what I found?"

"I'll look them over later. For now, why don't you just give me the highlights? I'm mainly interested in anything about Victor Perry you think could be relevant to this case."

"Okay," she said, sitting forward in her chair, "as you might guess, Victor has an impressive resume. He graduated from college with honors and went on to get his master's degree. However, that's probably not relevant to whether or not he's selling Falcon's secrets. What I believe is important is his character. That's why I concentrated on his email account and the way he communicates with people, especially his fellow workers."

"Okay. What's the bottom line there?"

"He argues with them a lot. If someone doesn't agree with him, he defends his position and refuses to listen to their point of view. And, he's not above putting them down for thinking a certain way. He can sound pretty mean, even revengeful in some of his emails."

"I'm curious how you think this plays into his willingness to sell company secrets."

"In my opinion, it could play a big role. If he isn't in agreement with the direction Falcon is going, he might decide to get revenge on his superiors by divulging proprietary information for money."

"You make a good point, Ashley."

She looked pleased as I opened up my laptop and typed a couple of things on the agenda document. "Anything else?"

"Yes, there's one more thing. Just give me a second to find it."

When Ashley was looking down at her notes, I used the opportunity to scrutinize her a little more closely.

Today, she had her hair pulled back away from her face, and she was wearing a tailored business suit, a look that made her appear older than she did at Cal's Coffee Café a few days ago, and I wondered if that was her intention. Did she want to make an impression on the division heads at the SAS meeting?

"Okay, here it is," she said. "In this email, a colleague is inviting Victor to join the baseball team he's putting together for the company picnic. It's a co-ed team, and he tells Victor he and his wife could be on the same team together. In the email, Victor refuses his invitation, and then he says some derogatory things about his wife."

I shook my head. "I don't remember seeing that email. What's the date on that?"

"It was back in March of this year." She put her notes down on the desk and looked up at me. "I thought you were having me review the materials on the flash drive so you wouldn't have to do it. Did you also go through these materials?"

I smiled at her and nodded. "Haven't you heard the saying two heads are better than one? Yes, I went through the materials on the flash drive, but I still wanted your perspective on Victor. I figured it would be different than mine, and that's exactly what's happened. I didn't give the emails much attention, but you concentrated on them and discovered some things I didn't."

She picked up her notes again. "I see your point. I concentrated on the emails because I thought they were very insightful. Of course, I'll be interested to hear your take on Victor as well."

"I'll do that in a minute." I gestured at the papers in her hand. "But first, why don't you finish telling me what kind of derogatory things Victor said about his wife."

"He said his wife hated baseball, which I guess isn't that derogatory, but then he said, and I'm quoting here, 'My wife isn't coordinated enough to play sports or do much else for that matter. All she's good at is cooking meals and taking care of the house.' "

"Maybe Victor was being sarcastic, you know, just kidding around with the guy, joking with him. That's hard to tell in an email."

"Maybe so, but to me it shows his character, and that's what's at stake here. I don't believe a man should ever put down his wife, even in a joking manner." She motioned toward me. "I'm sure you never did that to your wife."

"Uh . . . no, you're right," I said, giving her a weak smile. "I never did that to Emma, but she wouldn't have put up with it if I had."

◆ ◆ ◆ ◆

I thought Ashley probably sensed I was a little disconcerted by her mentioning my wife. Perhaps that was the reason she quickly went on to ask me what I'd learned about Victor.

I said, "I was interested in Victor's work history. If an employee doesn't show loyalty to his company, it's often because he changes jobs frequently. That could be the case with Victor since he's had four different jobs in the last twelve years."

"I can see why that might be a factor. Will you be contacting his former employers to see if they ever suspected Victor of giving away trade secrets while he was employed there?"

"Possibly. That depends on whether we turn up any tangible evidence of his disloyalty."

I glanced over at my computer for a second. "Another thing I looked at was Victor's outside interests. The biographical information in his personnel record listed his hobbies as baseball, bowling, and model airplanes."

"I noticed that myself. It made me wonder if the man in the pickup with Victor could be a model airplane enthusiast. Maybe that's what they were discussing."

"Or they could have been talking about baseball or bowling."

She smiled. "Or he could have been making arrangements to sell him the formula for XLM-15."

Even though I already knew the man in the parked vehicle was an ex-con named Devin Snead, I decided not to share that information with Ashley. I had two reasons for not doing so.

First, I didn't want her to announce she had that information prior to my division heads hearing it from Norwell.

If that happened, they might think I was giving Ashley preferential treatment because of who her father was. Even though I had the right to do so—I was their boss after all—managing their personalities was challenging enough without adding favoritism to the mix.

Second, I wanted Norwell to get the credit for discovering Snead's identity. He often took a backseat to others in our meetings, and I saw this as an opportunity to give him some kudos.

I said, "Yeah, that's what Victor might have been doing, all right. We'll know more once we put him under surveillance and decide how to handle Victor's case."

I glanced down at my watch. "Thanks, Ashley. Unless you have something else, I'll see you in the conference room at eleven."

When she stood up, she pointed at her notes. "Shall I leave these?"

"Please do. I'll definitely read them before the meeting."

A few minutes after she left, I put the finishing touches on the SAS agenda documents and buzzed Claudia to let her know the package was ready for her to make copies.

When she walked in my office, she didn't look happy.

"Don't blame me if Ms. Ashley Davenport showed up at your door without being announced. She never bothered to stop at my desk. She just breezed right past me while I was busy on the phone."

"Don't worry about it. She mentioned you were on the phone. Besides, I was expecting her anyway."

"Be that as it may," she said, flipping her hand in the air, "that woman really needs to show more respect for office protocol. She can't just sashay in here anytime she wants."

I handed her the documents. "Why do I have the feeling you might be reminding Ms. Ashley Davenport of that?"

She rolled her eyes and left without saying a word.

# Chapter 11

The conference room on the third floor of DCSS headquarters was the largest conference room in the building and could accommodate as many as thirty people.

However, the solid wooden table in the middle of the room could only seat fourteen—six on each side and two at each end.

There were additional chairs against the wall, but no one was sitting there today.

At one end of the room was a mobile TV cart with a mounted large screen television set, and next to it was a smaller version of the conference table, often used as a buffet table when a catered meal was on the agenda.

Today, it held soft drinks, bottled water, and two carafes of coffee.

At the other end of the conference room was a large interactive touchscreen used for presentations as well as brainstorming sessions.

When I entered the room, Mike Norwell was at the far end of the table hooking his computer up to the interactive screen.

The head of Cybersecurity, Luke Woodley, who replaced Norwell when he became my deputy, was seated to Norwell's right. The two men appeared to be in deep discussion about something.

When I sat down at the other end of the table, the head of Background Searches, Felicia Dean, was already in her usual seat in the middle of the table on my right. She nodded at me.

"Hi, Silas. I hope it's okay if I leave early. Before I got the call from Claudia, I'd already scheduled a luncheon appointment."

"That shouldn't be a problem, Felicia. This case probably won't involve your division anyway."

When I arrived at DCSS, it hadn't taken me but a few months to realize Felicia Dean hated meetings. I had to give it up to her, though. She always managed to come up with new excuses to get out of them.

Grant Edman, the head of Industrial Espionage, plopped himself down in the chair beside me. "No, Felicia, you won't be involved in this one. According to my sources, this case is all about industrial espionage, so I'm guessing my people will be up to bat for this one."

I gave Edman a smile. "Well, Grant, your sources could be wrong about this case. Discovering what this case is about is our first order of business today."

A few minutes later, Ashley came in the room and took a seat beside Felicia, who greeted her enthusiastically and immediately asked her how her father was doing.

Since at least half of Felicia's workload at DCSS was running background searches for Precept Healthcare, I found her affectionate attitude toward Ashley entirely understandable.

But, to be fair, Felicia was also a gregarious person.

When Ashley glanced over at me, I realized I'd been staring at her, so I gave her a nod, and she gave me a small wave.

The last person to arrive at the meeting was Buck Greiner. Trailing behind him was Jacob Javits, plus three interns, all males.

Because we seldom had a case that didn't require Greiner setting up surveillance on a target, he always brought his interns to a new case meeting with him. He said he preferred they hear about the case together. That way, he didn't have to repeat the details to each one.

Greiner and his interns sat down on the left side of the table next to Edman, but Javits took the chair next to Ashley.

"It looks like we're all here except Tyler," I said, "but he's in Oklahoma City today, so he can't make it."

I picked up the agenda packet Claudia had prepared for me. "As you can see from the documents Claudia sent out with your agenda, our newest client is Falcon Aeronautics. I'd like to begin the meeting today by describing the appointment I had with Richard Neal, Falcon's CEO, yesterday."

As soon as I started speaking, Norwell projected a photograph of Falcon's facilities on the interactive screen, and later, when I was talking about the photograph Neal took of Perry in his pickup in the grocery store parking lot, he put that picture up on the screen.

I said, "Before I begin my synopsis of what Neal told me about Victor Perry and his concerns about him, I need to preface my remarks by letting you know I took our newest intern, Ashley Davenport, with me to the appointment."

When Ashley heard her name, she glanced up from her iPad and smiled at everyone.

Once I finished outlining the scope of the investigation, I said, "When you reference this case in your reports, please use VP-489 as your file number. As I said, our primary objective is to determine whether Perry is selling Falcon's trade secrets to an interested party, and our first step toward accomplishing that objective is to identify the Unknown in the photograph Neal took in the parking lot."

I gestured at Norwell at the other end of the table. "Mike has already been able to get that information for us, so I'll turn the meeting over to him, and he can tell us what he learned."

Norwell cleared his throat, moved over to the interactive screen, and touched an icon. A few seconds later, a picture of Devin Snead's mug shot appeared on the screen.

I heard a few murmurs in the room, but it was Javits who blurted out, "Oh, wow, the Unknown has a record."

"That's right," Norwell said. "I was able to identify the man in Perry's vehicle as Devin Snead, the owner of a pawn shop on the south side of Dallas. This picture was taken when he was arrested for trafficking in stolen property. That was six years ago, and he ended up serving time—well, it was only eight months—but according to police records, he hasn't been arrested again since his release."

"What's he doing now?" Buck asked.

"I was just about to tell you that, Buck," Norwell said, shaking his head at Greiner's impatience. "He still runs the pawn shop. It's Goldie's Pawn Shop on Kimble Avenue, and he's listed as the owner."

Edman said, "A pawnbroker is hardly the type of person we usually encounter when we're investigating industrial espionage."

Everyone murmured their agreement with Edman's statement.

I said, "Hold on, everyone. Before we start discussing the different aspects of this case, I believe Mike has found out a few more things about Snead that might be relevant to our investigation."

He nodded. "Although Snead hasn't been arrested since he got out of jail, he was questioned by the police two years ago when his neighbor's husband was murdered. They never filed charges against him, but the case is still open."

Norwell touched the screen again and said, "I also ran Snead and Perry through various databases looking for some kind of connection between the two men. The only thing that popped up was baseball. It turns out both men have season tickets to the Rangers games. Of course, I'm talking about the professional baseball team."

Woodley shook his head. "I can't believe you got into that database. Maybe we need to ask Austin to get in touch with the Rangers management and suggest they hire us for their cybersecurity needs."

Buck gestured at Woodley. "Oh, give it up, Luke. We all know why you'd like to be in charge of the Rangers cybersecurity. You want to meet some of their players, have them sign something, and auction their autographs off to the highest bidder on the internet."

Woodley laughed. "Who, me?"

I tried to steer everyone back toward the matter at hand.

"This is probably a good time for us to discuss Victor Perry. Falcon's CEO gave us access to his personnel record and company email account, so as you can see from the materials I printed out for you, in some ways, Perry fits the profile of someone who'd be willing to sell his company's proprietary information."

The room was quiet for a few moments as everyone looked over a summary of Perry's biographical information.

Then, the discussion began.

◆ ◆ ◆ ◆

Basically, I just listened as each person made suggestions and argued their points—the interns said nothing—but when Felicia stood up and excused herself for her lunch appointment, I finally spoke up.

"Okay, if I'm hearing everyone correctly, you all agree Snead and Perry need to be put under surveillance. That's step one in determining if he's involved in selling Falcon's secrets. Buck, do you have any comments about that?"

Buck looked up from his legal pad where he was taking notes. "No doubt about it. Surveillance has to be the first step in this investigation. I'll set everything up and get started today."

"I promised Tomlin I'd be personally involved in this case," I said, "so go ahead and put Ashley and me on one of your teams. I'm available to do one rotation on Friday."

"Will do."

I continued, "I agree with everyone who expressed skepticism that a person like Devin Snead could be involved in industrial espionage, but since there's a possibility he could be acting as a broker for someone else, I believe we should explore that further."

Edman spoke up. "That's also what I think. Corporate spying is becoming so lucrative, everyone's getting in on it, so I wouldn't be surprised if that were true about Snead as well."

I waved my hand in Norwell's direction. "Mike, you said you dug up some other information on Victor Perry to share with us. Do you want to do that now?"

"Sure. It's just personal stuff, and I don't know whether it's relevant or not, but when I looked up whether Victor had any legal proceedings against him, I discovered he and his wife, Fran, had a brief separation three years ago. She was the one who filed the legal separation, but they got back together six months later, and she stopped the proceedings."

I said, "When Ashley went through Victor's emails, she discovered he said some rather unkind things about his wife, so perhaps those emails took place during the time they were separated."

Ashley spoke up. "I called it to Silas's attention because I felt it indicated something about Victor's character. To me, it showed he wasn't a man of integrity."

"Yes," Edman said, "I've noticed many people willing to give away company secrets often have personal issues going on. That was a good call, Ashley."

Ashley smiled but didn't respond to Edman's remark.

Neither did I.

Instead, I tried to move the discussion along in case the other interns in the room suddenly got the idea it was okay for them to enter into the discussion.

Ordinarily, interns weren't supposed to speak, only listen.

I failed to mention that to Ashley.

I questioned whether it would have made any difference.

◆ ◆ ◆ ◆

After several other opinions were offered about whether a person's past actions were good indicators of whether they would sell out their company or not, Norwell waved his hand at the group.

"I have one more item that might have significance for this case. This one also concerns Victor and a legal proceeding."

I nodded. "Sure, Mike, go ahead."

"Two years ago, Victor's mother-in-law fell and broke her hip. A few days later, she died. She was living in a nursing home when she fell, so not long after her death, Victor and his wife brought a wrongful death suit against the nursing home. As a result of their lawsuit, the Perrys received a financial settlement from the company. The amount wasn't disclosed, but past settlements suggest it was probably in the millions of dollars."

Everyone in the room seemed stunned by Norwell's disclosure.

Me included.

No one said anything for a moment.

"If that's true," Edman finally said, "why would Victor be interested in selling confidential information to Falcon's competitors? I doubt if he needs the money."

"To state the obvious," Greiner said, shaking his head, "this case gets more interesting all the time."

Interesting?

Puzzling was more like it.

◆ ◆ ◆ ◆

After I dismissed the meeting, I asked Ashley to stay behind for a minute so I could discuss our surveillance assignment with her.

"I'll be tied up with another case tomorrow," I said, "so I won't be able to participate in a surveillance rotation, but I told Buck I'd be available on Friday. Will that work for you?"

"Are you kidding? Anything will work for me. Other than the training sessions at the PI Academy, plus the few times I've gone out with Jacob Javits, I haven't had any experience running surveillance on anyone."

"I suppose you know it's mostly sitting around and a lot of doing nothing.

She nodded. "Yeah, I've heard it's pretty boring. I know it's not like the movies portray it."

"You're right. There are certainly some adrenaline-spiking moments every now and then, but those are few and far between."

"Meanwhile, is there anything I could be researching about Perry or Snead? Now that I have my PI license, I've got access to all the law enforcement databases through the *IntelManifest* website. Maybe I could be doing some snooping around on there."

"Sure, feel free to do that." I gestured over at Mike, who was at the other end of the table shutting down the interactive screen. "You could also ask Mike if he has some data digging you could do for him. Some of the computer stuff he does takes a lot of time."

"Okay, that sounds good. When should I meet you on Friday?"

"I'm not sure. I'll give you a call tomorrow when I hear back from Buck about the schedule."

"Thanks. I'll look forward to it."

"So will I."

As I watched her walk away, I realized I actually meant it.

# Chapter 12

As it turned out, I wrapped up everything I needed to do with Hines Communications and Tommy Hines by four o'clock on Thursday, so I gave Greiner a call and asked him to update me on his surveillance of Perry and Snead from Wednesday evening.

"I'm glad you called. I was just about to call you."

"About the Victor Perry case?"

"That's right. When our SAS meeting adjourned yesterday, I assigned two surveillance teams to watch Snead and Perry. Although I don't have any earth-shaking news to report, I figured you'd like to watch some video clips from each of my teams."

"But nothing happened?"

"I didn't say nothing happened. Something happened in each instance. I'm just not sure how significant it is. Don't get the idea Snead and Perry met in the parking lot again, though. That's not what happened."

"Naturally, you've succeeded in making me curious, so send me the clips, and I'll take a look at them."

"They're on their way."

"Have you scheduled me for a surveillance rotation tomorrow?"

"Yes. You and Ashley will be watching Perry beginning at four o'clock tomorrow afternoon. It's the four to eight rotation. Javits and I will be doing surveillance of Snead at the same time."

"Sounds good. I'll give you a buzz after I've viewed the clips."

◆ ◆ ◆ ◆

Before I opened the email from Greiner, I called Ashley to let her know when to meet me tomorrow for our surveillance on Victor Perry.

"I wanted to let you know Buck has us on the schedule for tomorrow's surveillance rotation from four-to-eight. Why don't you plan to come by my office at three."

"Sure, that'll work. Oh, by the way, you were right about Mike letting me help him with some research."

"Did he put you to work?"

"Yes, he had me go through some data files on the Rangers season ticket holders, and I just got off the phone with him after giving him the results. I imagine he'll be getting in touch with you soon."

"You sound a little excited about it. Did you find something?"

"I think so."

I waited a moment.

When she didn't say anything, I asked, "Do you want to tell me about it?"

"Is that okay? I don't want Mike to think I told you before I told him. Of course, I'm not telling you before I told him, but if you said something to him, he wouldn't know that, and he would think I told you before I told him. Oh, wait a minute. I'm repeating myself. I'm sorry. Sometimes I do that when I get excited about something."

I chuckled a little. "I appreciate your sensitivity as well as your honesty. Let's do it this way. Are you in the building right now?"

"Yes, I'm in my office."

"Buck just sent me a surveillance video from the Perry case—not the whole thing, just some clips he found interesting—so why don't you come up to my office, and we can look at them together. While you're on your way, I'll give Mike a call and ask him to update me about everything."

"Sounds like a plan. I'll be there in a few minutes."

"You might want to—"

She hung up before I could suggest she might want to stop by Claudia's desk before she knocked on my door.

I decided it didn't matter.

Claudia was either going to handle Ashley, or Ashley was going to handle Claudia. What happened would happen. If I needed to do a little cleanup afterward, I would.

In the meantime, I decided I would stay out of it.

◆ ◆ ◆ ◆

When I got off the phone with Ashley, I texted Norwell and asked for an update on the Perry case, and he called me a few seconds later.

"Hi, Silas. I knew you were busy dealing with Tommy Hines and his case today, so I decided not to call you until you asked for an update. The bottom line is, I think I discovered how Victor Perry and Devin Snead know each other."

"Really? Okay, tell me about it."

"First, I appreciate your suggesting Ashley help me go through some of the data I accumulated on Perry and Snead. She actually did a very good job. The last thing I had her do was study the Rangers seating assignments for season ticket holders at Globe Life Field and pinpoint where Perry and Snead would be sitting at a game."

"Good idea, but don't tell me their seats are next to each other at the ballfield."

"Well no, not exactly next to each other, but they're both assigned to section 20, row 12. Victor is in seat 3, and Snead is in seat 6."

"That's really close. If the seats between them were unoccupied, I could see the two men striking up a conversation."

"Yeah, me too."

"Okay, let's suppose that's how they met. Unfortunately, that information doesn't get us any closer to figuring out if Perry is sharing Falcon's secrets with Snead."

"No. In fact, if you ask me, this information just makes it more likely the two guys got together so they could talk about baseball. I can't see what else they would have in common."

"True, but it isn't exactly baseball season right now."

"So you think we're back to square one?"

"I'll let you know after I've viewed the surveillance videos Buck just sent me. He said there was something interesting in them."

"We've both heard that before, haven't we? What Buck labels as interesting may be nothing more than his target stopping by a fast-food joint when he usually goes inside a restaurant to have a meal."

I let out a short laugh. "I don't think Buck's that bad, but I agree he tends to exaggerate a little, but I'm withholding judgment until I see if these clips meet my criteria for being interesting or not."

The moment I got off the intercom with Norwell, it buzzed again.

"Ms. Davenport is here to see you," Claudia said.

Evidently, round one of Ashley vs. Claudia was a win for Claudia.

◆ ◆ ◆ ◆

I met Ashley at the door and invited her to have a seat on the couch so we could look at Buck's video clips on my big screen TV.

While I took the armchair across from her, she sat down on the couch, and after adjusting her short skirt, she asked, "Did you talk to Mike yet?"

"Yes, I just spoke to him. He told me what your research on the Rangers seating chart turned up."

She smiled. "How about that?"

"Nice job. He seems to think Perry and Snead probably met at the ballpark, and I agreed with him. What about you?"

"Oh, yeah. That's definitely what I think. Otherwise, I can't see what a small-time criminal like Snead would have in common with someone like Perry."

I nodded. "You're right, so maybe their common interest was the reason they met in the parking lot."

"Their behavior still seems a little odd to me. Why not meet for coffee or have a meal together instead?"

"Perhaps Buck's surveillance video will answer that question."

I pointed the remote at the screen, but I hit the Pause button a few seconds later. "I'm not sure you know this, but the timestamp for surveillance videos will always be in the bottom right-hand corner. Do you see it there? This is a clip from 5:47 yesterday."

"Yes, Buck explained that to me last week, and he said the location of where the video was taken is displayed on the left side."

"You got it. As you can see, this video starts out at Falcon Aeronautics."

I started the clip again. The camera on the dashboard of the surveillance vehicle zoomed in on the subject—Victor Perry.

In the clip, Perry got in his pickup and left the Falcon parking lot.

Ashley and I watched in silence as he traveled at a moderate rate of speed down Legacy Drive, seemingly headed in the direction of his home address.

However, some ten miles later, he put on his right turn signal and pulled in the parking lot of a bowling alley. Buck's surveillance team drove past the bowling alley, circled back, and parked next door at a paint store.

"Are Perry and Snead meeting up again?" Ashley asked.

"No, I don't think so. I'm sure Buck would have told me that."

After sitting in the parking lot at the bowling alley for ten minutes, Perry started his pickup and pulled back into traffic on Legacy Drive. Twenty minutes later, he turned left on Custer Road, the street that led into his neighborhood, and then he made another left turn onto Mesa Oaks Road, where his house was located.

The video ended after that.

Ashley looked over at me and shook her head. "What was Victor doing? Why did he park in front of the bowling alley for ten minutes?"

"I have no idea. It's possible he thought he was being followed, but that's just speculation on my part. Let's watch the other video and see if it sheds any light on his behavior."

The next surveillance video started out at 5:04 in the afternoon in front of Goldie's Pawn Shop in south Dallas when we saw Devin Snead getting into his Chevy Suburban.

Snead headed north on I-75, exiting the freeway on Legacy Drive, which just happened to be the same street where the bowling alley was located, the one where Perry was parked.

At 6:02, Snead drove past the bowling alley, briefly glanced over at the parking lot, and continued driving.

After taking Legacy Drive up to Custer Road—the street that led into Perry's neighborhood—he turned right instead.

From there, he got back on I-75.

That's where the video ended.

However, a short clip immediately followed that one. It showed Devin Snead returning to the neighborhood where his pawn shop was located and entering the Mexican restaurant next to it.

According to the time clock, it was 6:53.

When I stopped the video, Ashley threw her hands up in the air. "What was that about? Snead leaves his neighborhood, drives to North Dallas, turns around, and comes back to his neighborhood again. Why would he make a meaningless two-hour trip?"

"That's what it looks like to us, but I'm not sure it was a meaningless trip to Snead, or to Perry either for that matter."

"Do you think it was a dry run, some sort of a rehearsal for a future event?"

"That's a possibility, or Snead could have gotten cold feet about meeting up with Perry again. If they're planning something illegal, Perry wouldn't be in nearly as much trouble as Snead would be if they got caught. I'm sure Snead knows that too."

"You mean because Snead has a criminal record?"

I nodded. "Yeah, and Perry probably has enough money to hire himself a top-notch lawyer; whereas I doubt if Snead can afford one."

"Do you happen to know which one of these men Buck wants us to follow tomorrow?"

"We'll be tailing Victor Perry, and he and Jacob will be following Snead. I'll check with Buck in the morning and see if anything unusual happened with these guys today. This same scenario could have played itself out today, but I rather doubt it."

Ashley grabbed her purse. "Okay, I'll be here at three o'clock tomorrow afternoon. Thanks for letting me watch the videos with you."

Before she headed for the door, she gestured at me and said, "When we finish our surveillance rotation tomorrow, would you like to go grab a bite to eat together?"

I wasn't anticipating the question.

Otherwise, I might have come up with a good excuse.

Or maybe not.

"Sure, Ashley, I'd enjoy that."

◆ ◆ ◆ ◆

Once Ashley left, I sent the videos to Norwell, and then I called Greiner who was with Javits in the parking lot at Falcon Aeronautics, waiting for Perry to exit the building.

"I won't keep you but a minute, Buck, but I wanted you to know I just watched the video clips, and you were right; I found them very interesting."

"Yeah, I thought you would. There's something weird going on with those guys, but I haven't figured out what it is yet."

"Me neither, but I agree with you."

"Should I send the videos to Mike or do you want to do that?"

"I've already done it. By the way, Mike thinks he knows how Perry and Snead met. He discovered their Rangers seat assignments are in the same row at Globe Life Field."

"Is that right? Well, there you go then. Only a nerdy guy like Mike would be able to figure that out."

I decided not to comment on his remark.

"I'll let you go now, Buck, but I'll be including your clips in my latest update to everyone, as well as the stuff Mike sent me."

"Before you hang up, Silas, I need to ask you something."

"Sure. Go ahead."

"I was thinking of getting in touch with our detective friend, Marcus Nixon, and asking him if he would be willing to do some research for us about Devin Snead. Would you be okay with that?"

"Hmmm. Maybe."

I paused a beat. "I'll tell you what, Buck. I'll give him a call myself."

"You sure? I don't mind doing it."

"I'm sure. I'll let you know what he says. If I don't call you back tonight, you'll know I didn't catch him."

Marcus Nixon was a detective in the Dallas Police Department, North Central Division, and his wife, Luisa, was employed at DCSS in Personnel. Like me, they were also members of Crossroads Church. Nixon was usually more than willing to help me out if I discovered criminal activity was going on while I was investigating a case of corporate security, or if I had questions related to police matters.

Since Nixon preferred to get a text message instead of a phone call, I sent him a text and asked him to call me when he had a chance.

As I was getting in my car for the drive home, he texted me back and said he'd have to call me tomorrow unless it was an emergency.

I texted him back. *"Not an emergency. Just need info on Devin Snead and/or Goldie's Pawn Shop."*

*"Sounds familiar. Call you tomorrow."*

Tomorrow was scheduled to be a busy day.

And to top it off, I said I'd end the day by having dinner with Ashley. How did that happen?

# PART FOUR

# Chapter 13

*Friday, December 2*

I didn't get a call back from Detective Marcus Nixon until midmorning on Friday, and when my cell phone rang, I had just sent my division heads an update on VP-489.

Other than the surveillance clips on Snead and Perry from Wednesday afternoon and Mike's info about how the two men could have met each other, there wasn't anything new to report.

Buck's surveillance on the men from Thursday had been a dud.

Neither one of them had done anything out of the ordinary.

"Hi, Silas. How's it going? Sorry I couldn't get back with you yesterday. Things were a little hectic around here."

"Not a problem. I won't keep you long, Marcus, but if you have time, I wonder if you'd mind running someone through the system. He's recently popped up on our radar over here at DCSS."

"You're talking about Devin Snead, right? I thought that name sounded familiar when you texted me, or rather the pawn shop did, so I did a quick search this morning, and I was right about that. The pawn shop isn't in my district, but I've heard our guys talk about it before."

"Would you mind telling me what you know about the pawn shop? And if you looked into Snead's record, I'd like to hear that as well."

"I can tell you Devin Snead served time—at least a few months—and he's also friendly with some questionable people."

"We've been watching Snead in connection with a possible corporate espionage case. Would the questionable people you mentioned have connections in the aerospace or aeronautics world?"

He laughed. "Are you kidding? I doubt if Snead would even know the meaning of those words. When I say questionable people, I'm talking about the Campo crime family. They're mostly into drugs and gambling, but they've also been tied to some high-profile murder cases as well as several robberies in the Highland Park area."

"And Snead runs with that crowd?"

"No, not really. Let's just say he's loosely connected to them. From what I can tell, he's mostly a freelance guy who looks for opportunities to make a buck, legally or illegally, and who's smart enough to stay off the police blotter."

"You consider him a petty criminal, then? Relatively harmless?"

"For the most part, yeah. He did show up as a suspect in a homicide investigation two years ago, but he was never charged."

"Would you mind telling me why Snead was considered a suspect? Could you just give me the highlights of the case?"

"Be glad to. The victim was a white male who lived a block away from Snead and was shot during an apparent robbery attempt. The victim's wife was upstairs, and she said she didn't know what was going on until she heard the shot. When the neighbors were questioned about seeing anyone at the house, one couple mentioned Devin Snead and his wife were good friends of the victim and his wife, and they'd seen Snead at the victim's house earlier in the day, but the wife hadn't said anything to the police about him being there."

"Yeah, that *does* sound a little suspicious, especially since the wife didn't mention Snead being there, but of course, she could have been in shock. That might have explained it."

"Sure, that's possible. Snead was brought in for questioning, but he claimed he was at the house delivering a couple of tickets to a Rangers game that he wasn't going to use. Sure enough, a couple of tickets were found in the victim's billfold."

"You said it was an *apparent* robbery attempt?"

"Yeah, the only thing missing was the victim's cell phone."

"That's strange."

"But here's the kicker. The husband had a million-dollar insurance policy on himself, which means, the wife is sitting pretty now."

"Hmmm. Interesting."

"That's all I was able to dig up on the guy, Silas. I hope it helps with your case. I'm sorry, but I gotta run now."

"Thanks, Marcus. I don't know whether it helps us or not, but I appreciate you looking into it for me."

"Sure thing. You doing okay? You sound better than the last time I talked to you."

"You know how it is—good days and bad days. The last few days have been pretty good, though."

◆ ◆ ◆ ◆

Ashley and I arrived in the parking lot of Falcon Aeronautics shortly before four o'clock. As soon as we were in place, I let the other surveillance team know we were there, and they left the area a few minutes later.

Falcon's research facilities were housed in a four-story building a quarter of a mile from where we met with Richard Neal on Tuesday, but since the parking lot was located at the front of the research building, we had an excellent view of the entire complex.

However, I'd already spotted Perry's red pickup. It was two rows away from where we were parked, so I didn't figure there was much chance of us missing him when he got off work.

Once I finished texting the other team, I pointed down at the backpack at Ashley's feet. "I see you came prepared to stay awhile."

She smiled as she picked up the bag from the floorboard. "I wasn't sure whether you would bring your own provisions or not, so I brought enough water and snacks for both of us."

She pulled out a bottled water. "Would you like one now?"

"No thanks. You don't have any coffee in there, do you?"

"As a matter of fact, I do."

She reached in and brought out a stainless steel thermos.

I shook my head when she offered it to me. "No, thanks. I was just checking to be sure you hadn't forgotten the essentials."

I reached across the backseat and grabbed my own bag. "It's always good to have water and snacks, but the main thing you need for a stakeout is a camera equipped with a zoom lens. Plus, I also carry a set of binoculars with me."

"What? No parabolic mic?"

"It's in the trunk."

She laughed.

We sat there for a few moments without saying anything.

Just before it got awkward, she turned to me and asked, "Anything new on the case?"

"Oh, I'm sorry. I meant to tell you earlier, but then you made the comment about my clothes, and I forgot about it."

When Ashley and I were leaving the DCSS building, she said she was surprised to see me wearing jeans today. When I pointed out DCSS allowed its employees to observe casual Friday, she said, "Yes, I knew that. That's why I'm wearing jeans today, but to be truthful, you don't strike me as the casual dresser type."

"Ordinarily, I'm not, but when I'm running surveillance on a target, I usually don't wear a suit. That is, unless the occasion calls for it. That way, if I have to leave my vehicle for any reason, I can easily blend into the crowd."

I pointed over to my silver Toyota 4Runner.

"That's also the reason I drove my SUV today. I primarily use it for surveillance purposes because my Lexus would stick out like a sore thumb in a company's parking lot or other similar locations."

"That makes sense, but I certainly hope you didn't take my comment the wrong way. You look nice all the time."

As soon as she said that, I realized I hadn't heard a woman say something about what I was wearing since Emma passed away. Thinking about it distracted me for several minutes, and consequently, I forgot all about giving Ashley the update on the case.

Now, as we waited for Perry to exit the building, I said, "There's been a few interesting developments in the case since we talked yesterday, but since I haven't had a chance to update Buck about them, if you don't mind, I'll give him a call and tell you both at the same time."

"No, I don't mind. Go ahead. I'm eager to hear them."

When Buck answered his phone, he also sounded eager to hear them, but before I could tell him, he asked, "Have you seen any sign of Perry yet?"

"No, but Neal said he usually leaves work around five-thirty."

"Yeah, that's what's been happening the last couple of days. I was just wondering, because Snead came out of the pawn shop a few minutes ago and put some kind of canvas bag in his vehicle like he was about to leave, but now he's gone back inside."

"I seem to remember it was about this time on Wednesday that Snead left the pawn shop and drove up here to North Dallas. Are we about to have a repeat performance?"

"I guess we'll know in a few minutes. Go ahead with your update. I've got you on speaker so Javits can hear you."

I spent the next fifteen minutes telling them about my conversation with Marcus Nixon and what he found out about Devin Snead and his criminal past.

When I finished, Buck said, "Well, one thing's for sure, if Snead is involved in industrial espionage, he's managed to move up several rungs on the criminal ladder. This isn't small-time stuff."

"Yeah, but I'm beginning to have my doubts this case has anything to do with Perry selling company secrets."

Buck didn't say anything for a few seconds, but then I heard him ask Javits, "What's he doing there?"

I wasn't able to hear Javits' answer, but Buck got back on the phone a few seconds later and said, "Are you ready for this? Snead just came out of the pawn shop and slapped a magnetic sign on the door of his Chevy Suburban. You know the kind I'm talking about?"

"Like a temporary business sign they use on work vehicles?"

"That's right. This one appears to be an electrician's sign—Eddie's Electrical Service. Okay, now he's leaving the parking lot. I need to go, but as soon as I know where he's heading, I'll text you."

"Wow," Ashley said, after I disconnected the call, "I didn't realize this case would be so complicated."

"You and me both."

◆ ◆ ◆ ◆

Fifteen minutes later, Buck texted me and said Snead was on I-75 going north again, possibly toward our area. About the same time, I saw several Falcon employees exiting the building.

Perry was among them.

He headed straight for his pickup and didn't talk to anyone.

As I quickly assessed his appearance, I noted he wasn't carrying anything in his hands, nor did he appear to be armed.

"There's Victor," Ashley said, a few seconds later. "He's leaving the building now."

"What can you tell me about him?"

"Uh . . . he's walking pretty fast, and he's not paying attention to the people around him."

"Anything else?"

"Let's see. He's dressed in a yellow sports shirt and beige khakis. Oh, and he's wearing a pair of brown loafers."

"What else?"

"Mmm. I'm not sure. Did I miss something?"

I started my SUV as Perry got in his pickup. "Did he have a briefcase or a backpack with him? Could you tell if he had a weapon on him?"

She thought about my question for a few seconds. "No, he didn't have a backpack or a briefcase. His shirt was tucked in, and he wasn't wearing a jacket, so I don't believe he was carrying."

"If you only have three seconds to make an assessment about him, which one of the things that you mentioned would you consider to be the most important one?"

She hung her head for a second. "I really should have noticed whether he was carrying. That was dumb of me, wasn't it?"

"Nothing is dumb if you learn a lesson from it."

"We were definitely taught how to be observant at the PI Academy, but putting those lessons into practice is a lot easier said than done."

"Well, to be fair, I've had a lot more practice at this than you have. There were times when I was on a covert assignment for the DIA that my life depended on making those judgments in three seconds, so believe me, I learned that lesson pretty quick."

We both stopped talking for a moment while we watched to see which direction Perry would turn once he came to the intersection.

He turned right on Legacy Drive.

"Is he going to the bowling alley again?" she asked.

"Since Snead is also traveling this direction, I believe there's a good chance the two of them are about to meet up again, but whether their rendezvous point is the bowling alley, I couldn't say."

Ten minutes later, we had our answer.

Perry made a right turn into the bowling alley.

I kept driving, turned at the next intersection, and came back to the bowling alley, parking the Toyota four rows away from Perry's pickup. The parking space I chose made it easy for me to see into the truck's rear window by using the telephoto lens on my camera.

My objective was to see if Perry was on the phone with someone.

After grabbing my camera, I handed the binoculars to Ashley and explained what I was doing.

"He's just sitting there," she said, as she adjusted the focus on the glasses. "He's not on his phone."

"No, I personally believe he's waiting for Snead."

Ashley was leaning forward in her seat, completely tensed up.

I suppose that was the reason she jumped when my cell phone vibrated. The caller was Buck.

"Snead just got off the interstate on Legacy Drive," he said. "I'm sure he's heading to the bowling alley. What's happening with Perry?"

"He's already at the bowling alley. You can't miss his pickup. It's near the front door, and we're in my Toyota four rows behind him."

"Copy that. I believe something's going down today, Silas. If they head off together, you take the lead, and I'll bring up the rear."

About ten minutes after Buck hung up, Snead arrived.

Unlike the previous day, Snead parked his Suburban fairly close to where Perry was parked, and seconds later, he walked over and got inside his pickup.

"I believe Snead's carrying," Ashley said, lowering the binoculars for a moment. "He's wearing a jacket, but when he got inside the pickup, I'm sure I caught a glimpse of his side holster."

"Good call. I believe you're right."

I wished she wasn't right, but she was.

◆ ◆ ◆ ◆

Suddenly, I felt apprehensive about the situation. For one thing, I realized there was only a remote chance VP-489 had anything to do with corporate espionage.

Instead, I was fairly certain Snead and Perry had partnered up to engage in some sort of criminal activity.

With that in mind, I found myself getting anxious about whether Ashley was experienced enough to handle things if the situation got out of hand, turned ugly, or went sideways.

Would I be able to protect her if that happened?

The last time I tried to protect a woman in my care from some unseen danger, I was a miserable failure.

Now, I found myself doing something I hadn't been able to do in the last six months—I prayed and asked God to give me wisdom and guidance.

I silently screamed out to him for help.

He answered the way he always answered me in the past—especially during several terrifying moments in Afghanistan, as well as that awful day when Emma received her diagnosis—he gave me a calming sense of peace.

Now, as I watched Buck park his vehicle a few spaces away from mine, I felt less afraid and more at ease.

"What's Perry giving Snead?" Ashley asked. "I can't make it out."

I focused the zoom lens on what was happening in the cab of the pickup where Perry had removed something from his shirt pocket.

"It looks like a photograph of someone," I said.

"Yes, and they must be discussing the person in the photograph because Perry keeps pointing at it."

As I snapped several frames with my camera, Snead placed the photograph in his jacket pocket, got out of Perry's pickup, climbed back in his Suburban, and drove off a few seconds later.

Buck let him have a head start, gave us a brief nod, and left the parking lot behind him.

Seconds later, much to my surprise, Perry exited his pickup carrying a bowling bag.

Then, he strolled across the parking lot and into the bowling alley.

"Are we going to follow him?" Ashley asked.

"I don't think so," I said, looking down at the images on my camera.

"Why not? Don't you want to see if he's meeting someone?"

"No, I'm not concerned about Perry. I'm more concerned about Snead. I want to know who he's about to meet."

I turned the camera around so Ashley could see the LCD screen and view the shot I'd just taken of the photograph Perry had given Snead.

"Do you recognize this person?" I asked.

Ashley studied the image for a moment. "I believe that's Victor's wife, Fran. That same photograph was on the flash drive Neal's assistant gave us."

Her eyes widened as she looked across the seat at me.

"Why would Victor give Devin Snead a photograph of his wife?"

"I'm not sure, but I have a feeling we better find out pretty quick."

# Chapter 14

Just before I pulled out of the parking lot of the bowling alley, I called Buck and put him on speakerphone.

"Where's Snead now?" I asked.

"He's on Legacy, and he's coming up on Custer Road. I'm guessing he'll get on the freeway and head back to the pawn shop."

"FYI. Perry just went inside the bowling alley."

"Hmmm. I suppose you'll be stuck there for a couple of hours."

"No, I'm on Legacy Drive, a few miles behind you."

"Why did you—"

"I doubt if you were able to see it from where you were parked, but when Snead and Perry were inside his pickup, Perry gave him a picture of his wife. I find that very troubling."

"Uh . . . yeah. I'd say so. What's going on there?"

"I suppose there could be a logical explanation for his behavior, but I haven't come up with one yet, even in the best scenario."

"Well, if your worst case scenario includes Snead paying a visit to Perry's house, then I'm sorry to tell you he just turned left on Custer Road. He's not getting back on the expressway."

He paused. "Oh, wait a second. He also just turned left on Mesa Oaks Road into Perry's neighborhood. Shall I follow him in there?"

"Are you able to keep an eye on him without drawing attention to yourself?"

"I think so. I'm pulling up in front of a house three doors down from Perry's driveway, so let's hope the owners aren't at home right now."

"At the moment, I'm at the intersection of Legacy and Custer, so I should be there in a few minutes. What's Snead doing now?"

"He's getting out of the Suburban, and he's carrying the canvas bag we saw him put in his vehicle before he left the pawnshop. Now he's walking up to Perry's front door."

After I made the turn onto Mesa Oaks Road, I drove past where Buck's vehicle was parked, but I slowed down as I rolled past Perry's house, where Snead was at the front door talking to Fran, Perry's wife.

She was holding the door open for him.

Once I pulled my SUV to the curb two houses down, I asked Buck, "I suppose you saw Fran let him into the house?"

"Unfortunately, yes. Now what?"

"Good question."

◆ ◆ ◆ ◆

For the next few minutes, Buck and I sat there in our vehicles and went over some ideas about how to handle the situation.

Javits and Ashley didn't say a word, but when I brought up the idea of one of us going up to the door and pretending to be a salesman just to see if everything appeared to be okay inside, Ashley spoke up.

"Why don't I do that? I could act like I was the next-door neighbor, and I needed to borrow something."

"No," I said, "I don't think that—"

"Yeah," Buck said, "that's probably the best idea. If something's wrong and Fran sees you, then she'll know you're not a neighbor, and she could try to signal you or something."

"That's a little dangerous, don't you think?" Javits said. "I mean dangerous for Ashley as well as Perry's wife."

Ashley patted her purse. "Not to worry. I have my pistol with me."

Buck was in total agreement.

As much as I hated to admit it, it *was* a pretty good idea, but I wasn't about to let Ashley do it alone.

"I agree this might work," I said, "but I'm coming with you. I'll stay out of sight around the corner there by the front door. Whoever comes to the door won't see me."

"Okay," Buck said. "Meanwhile, Jacob and I will be watching everything from here, ready to move if the situation looks like it's getting out of hand."

"Agreed." I paused for a moment. "No, Buck, on second thought, I have an assignment for Jacob."

"Sure, Silas," Jacob said, a note of eagerness in his voice. "What is it? What's my assignment?"

"I'd like for you to get Detective Marcus Nixon on the phone—Buck will give you his number—and let him know what's happening. Tell him we might need his assistance if we run into a problem."

"Will do," he said. "I can handle that."

"Buck," I said, "I'm putting my phone in my pocket now, but I won't disconnect our call. That way, you'll know what's going on."

"Copy that. I'm going silent now."

I slipped my phone inside my jacket pocket, unholstered my gun, chambered a round, and looked over at Ashley. "Are you sure you want to do this?"

"Absolutely."

"Let's do it then."

◆ ◆ ◆ ◆

I kept my gun at my side as Ashley and I walked over to Perry's ranch-style house, a red-brick structure with a three-car garage and a long front porch that stretched across the width of the house.

As she stood at the front door, I was to her right, pressed up against the brick wall where I was holding my gun at chest level.

I nodded at her, and she rang the doorbell.

I could hear the chime going off inside.

Whoever came to the door wouldn't be able to see me, nor I them, but I was counting on Ashley letting me know who answered the door.

Several things flashed through my head as I stood there. Most of them were things I wished I'd done before arriving at this point.

I wished I'd thought this thing through a little more.

I wished I'd cautioned Ashley not to unconsciously give my presence away by looking over at me if she got scared.

I wished I had taken more time to go over the story Ashley planned to give to the person who came to the door.

Did she even have a story? Did she even have a plan?

She reached over and rang the doorbell again.

I wasn't sure she should have done that.

It didn't matter.

The door swung open.

"Can I help you?"

Ashley didn't need to say anything to let me know who answered the door.

I immediately knew who it was.

It was a man's voice, a deep, gruff voice.

"Oh hi, sir," Ashley said.

Her voice was pitched a little higher than usual, which told me she was pretty nervous.

"Is uh . . . Fran around? I'm her next-door neighbor." Ashley motioned off to her left. "I thought she was probably here since I saw your repair truck in the driveway."

"Yeah, she's here, but she can't come to the door right now. Tell me what you want, and I'll give her a message."

"No, that's okay. Do you mind if I ask you what you're doing here?"

I immediately tensed up.

What was she thinking?

"I'm ah . . ."

"What I mean is, what kind of electrical work are you doing for Fran? When I was with her the other day, we both talked about wanting dimmer switches on the chandeliers in our dining rooms, and I was thinking if that's what you were doing here, maybe you could come over to my place and work on mine while you're here."

"That's right. I'm working on the lights in her dining room."

"So could you come over and see about mine while you're here?"

I had no idea what kind of reaction Snead was having to Ashley's questions, but he was becoming a lot slower about answering her questions, and now he wasn't saying anything.

I didn't consider that a good sign.

I figured that meant he was trying to decide what to do.

As Snead delayed answering her, Ashley took a step across the threshold as if she were about to enter the house.

"Fran," she yelled out, "is it okay if I come in and see what the electrician's doing in your dining room?"

"Yeah, lady," Snead said, grabbing her arm, "why don't you come in. The more the merrier."

The moment Snead grabbed Ashley's arm, I swung around the side of the house and leveled my gun at him.

"Don't do it, Snead. Let go of her."

Snead immediately released Ashley's arm, but then he turned and started running toward the kitchen area, where I presumed he was about to exit out the back door.

I followed him, and since I knew Buck was still listening in on our open phone line, I said, "Buck, I think Snead's coming your way. He's heading for the back door."

I wasn't able to hear Buck's response, but by then, I was in the kitchen where I found the door to the patio standing wide open, so I followed Snead outside.

He'd already made it across the backyard and was turning toward the street. Suddenly, Buck came running at him with his gun drawn.

"Hold it right there, mister," Buck said.

Snead stopped in his tracks and raised his hands.

A few feet behind Buck was Jacob, who was waving his phone in the air. "The police are on their way. I just talked to Marcus Nixon, and he should be here any minute."

"You've got to be kidding me," Snead said, shaking his head. "Did Victor set this whole thing up? Who are you people anyway?"

No one answered him.

I said, "Buck, I need to go inside and check on Ashley."

"Sure, go ahead. Meanwhile, Mr. Snead and I will go out to the curb and wait for our friends from the Dallas PD to show up."

I didn't see Ashley when I stepped back inside the kitchen.

However, I thought I heard voices toward the back of the house, and after clearing the living room, I walked down the hallway where the bedrooms were located and entered the master bedroom.

That's where I found Ashley.

She was sitting on the king-size bed untying some cords from around Fran's wrists. Fran's ankles were also tied together.

I heard Fran gasp as I entered the room, and I quickly holstered my gun and started untying the cords around her ankles.

"It's okay, Fran," Ashley said. "Don't worry. This is Silas McKay, and I'm sure he's already taken care of Devin Snead."

"She's right," I said, removing the cords. "Don't worry about Snead. The police have him in custody now."

Ashley freed her wrists and said, "When I found her, this was around her mouth." She held up a strip of duct tape.

Fran immediately buried her face in her hands and started crying.

"I was so scared," she said, as the tears flowed. "I didn't know what he was planning to do to me. I was afraid I was about to die."

Ashley put her arm around her and told her everything was okay.

I sat there quietly until she seemed to get her emotions under control, and then I asked, "Had you ever seen Devin Snead before? Do you know the man who tied you up?"

"No, I don't know him. I didn't even know that was his name. When Victor—he's my husband—left for work this morning, he told me Eddie's Electrical Service would be out around five o'clock to fix one of the outlets in our kitchen that wasn't working. One day it was working, and the next day it wasn't. I thought that awful man was here to fix the outlet, and that's why I let him in the house."

"What happened after you let him in?"

"As soon as I closed the door, he grabbed me and tied my hands behind my back. Then he put some tape over my mouth and dragged me in here to the bedroom. He had just tied those cords around my ankles when the doorbell rang. At first, I didn't think he would go to the door, but then when it rang again, he left the room. I tried to make some noise, but I didn't think anyone would hear me."

It looked like Fran was about to start crying again, so I offered to get her some water. She quickly accepted my offer, and I headed to the kitchen. When I got there, I heard the front door open. "Silas, it's me, Marcus. Are you in here?"

"I'm in the kitchen," I said, poking my head around the corner.

"Where's Mrs. Perry? Is she okay?"

"She's a little shaken up, but she's okay. One of our female investigators is with her."

"Where is she?" he asked, as two uniformed police officers suddenly appeared in the doorway.

"She's in the master bedroom. That's where Snead had her tied up. I just came in here to get her some water."

He gestured at the police officers. "One of these guys can take her the water. You and I need to talk about what happened here."

After I handed the glass of water to one of the policemen, Nixon motioned for me to follow him in the living room where he sat down in a recliner, and I took a seat on the couch.

"So bring me up to speed on things," he said, pulling out his cell phone. "What went down here?"

Nixon took notes on his phone as I told him about the transaction between Perry and Snead in the parking lot of the bowling alley and what happened after we followed Snead to Perry's house.

"I understand why you felt you couldn't wait for law enforcement to arrive," Nixon said after I finished, "and personally, I believe you made the right decision, but let's face it, that was a very dangerous situation. I'm just thankful no one got seriously injured."

"So am I. Do you know what's happening with Perry right now?"

"A couple of detectives are taking him in for questioning, but when I spoke with Devin Snead a few minutes ago, he immediately brought up Victor's name and accused him of setting him up. No doubt we'll learn more once we get them in an interview room."

"I probably don't need to ask you this, Marcus, but I'd like to be kept informed about the outcome of those interviews."

"You can be assured of that, brother. I'll give you a call as soon as I know something."

"Thanks, I appreciate it."

He smiled as he put away his phone. "It's good to see you, Silas. Maybe we can get together for lunch soon."

"I'd like that. Emma and I really enjoyed having lunch with you and Luisa after church on Sundays. To be honest, I miss those times."

"I'm off this weekend. Maybe we'll see you at church this Sunday."

"Yeah," I said, nodding my head, "maybe you will."

# Chapter 15

*Saturday, December 3*

When I woke up on Saturday morning, I had mixed feelings. On the one hand, I felt good about the job DCSS had done to keep Fran Perry out of danger, plus I was also happy I had been able to inform Richard Neal his company's secrets weren't being compromised, even though one of his researchers had been arrested.

On the other hand, although it was a short-lived experience, I was sorry Fran had to go through such a terrifying ordeal.

The fact that it happened to her in the first place made me wonder if I should have acted sooner, like knocked on her door as soon as we saw Snead entering her house.

During breakfast, as I was going over the whole thing in my head again—while also keeping an eye on the news to see if the media had picked up the story yet—I realized I may have been hesitant to take aggressive action because I was concerned about Ashley getting hurt.

That was foolish on my part.

Ashley more or less proved my worries were pointless when I saw her in action and observed how capable she was of handling herself and making quick decisions when the occasion called for it.

Granted, she *was* a little shaken up afterward.

In fact, on our way back to DCSS headquarters, when I suggested we might want to take a raincheck on having dinner together, she didn't argue with me, especially when I told her I needed to go talk to Austin Tomlin and update him on the case.

"Yes, let's do it another time," she said. "I don't think I would be very good company tonight."

"I can certainly understand why, but in case you're wondering, I think you did a good job today, Ashley. There aren't many interns here at DCSS who would have been able to maintain their cool under pressure like you did."

"I don't mind telling you I was pretty scared."

"Fear is seldom a bad thing. I believe God gave us that emotion for a reason. I confess, though, I often need to ask him for wisdom not to fear the wrong things."

She looked amused at my response. "I didn't realize you were a religious person, Silas."

"That isn't how I think of myself, but I *am* a believer."

"Is that right? What do you believe?"

I looked over at her. "You're asking me what I believe? Are you sure you want to hear it?"

She shrugged. "Sure, why not?"

"Well, the short version is I believe God created all things, and he's also sovereign over them. I believe he created man and put him on planet Earth to enjoy everything he created and to praise him for creating it. Man blew it, of course, but I believe God loved us so much he came to planet Earth in the form of a man so he could sacrifice his life to bring us back into a relationship with him. If we're willing to accept the sacrifice he made for us, then I believe that relationship is restored, and we'll get to spend our eternity with him in heaven."

"And what happens if we don't? Accept his sacrifice, I mean."

"Well, if we don't accept the sacrifice he made for us, I believe we're free to pay for our sins ourselves in a place that isn't called heaven, and we'll be paying that debt for an eternity."

She let out a short laugh. "And you don't call that being religious?"

"No, I call it having a relationship with Jesus."

I gave her a smile. "But don't get me wrong, Ashley. I'm really lousy at this relationship sometimes. For the past several months, I've been mad at God for taking Emma away from me, and I'm not sure I'm over it yet, but at least I'm working on it."

"Do you believe your wife's in heaven right now?"

"I'm sure of it."

She didn't say anything else to me until we said goodbye to each other after we arrived back at the DCSS building.

When I told her I'd see her on Monday unless I got a call from Detective Nixon, she said, "Feel free to call me anytime, Silas."

◆ ◆ ◆

After putting my breakfast dishes in the dishwasher, I made myself a fresh cup of coffee and walked in the living room to take another look at Marissa's Christmas tree.

My intention was to get some inspiration to go out and do some Christmas shopping for my DCSS staff, something Emma had always done for me.

However, the moment I sat down on the couch, I got a call from Nixon. "Good morning, Silas. Marcus Nixon here. Did I catch you at a bad time?"

"No, not at all. What's up?"

"I wanted to update you on what happened yesterday when we interrogated Devin Snead and Victor Perry. Of course, we aren't allowed to call it an interrogation anymore. Nowadays, we take suspects to interview rooms where we question them."

"I hear you. My question is, did you find out anything?"

"Oh, you bet we did. But we didn't learn anything from Victor. He lawyered up right away. Snead was a different story. He was hoping to cut a deal for himself, so he told us pretty much everything."

"That doesn't surprise me."

"The condensed version of what he said is that he and Victor met at a Rangers game a few years ago, and although he thought the guy was a nerd, Snead is an avid baseball fan, so he enjoyed talking to him."

"Some of us at DCSS figured that's how the two of them met. And yeah, I'm sure Snead thought Perry was a nerdy guy, all right."

"He said a couple of months after they met, Perry told him his wife was awarded a big settlement in a lawsuit, and he began making plans how to spend the money. Not long after that, he started complaining his wife didn't agree with him about what to do with the money."

"Uh-oh. Trouble in paradise. Instant wealth can do that."

"True. I've seen it before when someone wins the lottery. Well, anyway, when Perry started making noises about how he wished his wife would go to an early grave, Snead offered to make that happen for $100,000. Naturally, Snead told us he was only joking about it, but when Perry took him seriously, he decided to go along with it. Of course, he told us he wasn't really planning to go through with it. He was just going to take Perry's money and disappear."

"I'm sure that's the kind of defense Snead's lawyer will argue in court, but if that's what he was planning, then why was he armed, and why did he go to Perry's house and terrorize Fran?"

"Exactly. When we started asking those kinds of questions, that's when Snead called for his lawyer."

"So I suppose that put an end to your interrogation, or to be politically correct, your interview."

He chuckled. "Yeah, that ended the interview right there."

"Well, thanks for updating me, Marcus. I really appreciate it."

"You're more than welcome, Silas. I'll be coming by your office on Tuesday to take your statement. Maybe I'll have more to tell you then."

"I'll let Claudia know you'll be dropping by."

"Oh, please do. Otherwise, I won't get in to see you."

◆ ◆ ◆ ◆

After I got off the phone with Nixon, I paced around the living room trying to make up my mind about whether I should call Ashley immediately or wait and talk to her in person on Monday.

I decided to do both—call her and see her in person.

When she answered her phone, I asked her if I could take her to dinner so I could give her the latest details on the Perry case.

"You mean tonight?"

"Yes, if that's convenient for you. If not, I could just see you in the office on Monday."

"No, tonight's fine. I don't have any plans. Oh, I probably shouldn't have said that. I don't want you to think I don't have a social life."

"Don't worry. I'm sure that's not true."

She laughed. "You're right. I guess it's obvious I enjoy being around people. What time do you want to pick me up? Do you have my address? Do you know how to get to my place?"

"How about six o'clock? No, I haven't looked up your address, but if you want to give it to me now, I'm pretty sure I'll be able to find you."

"Of course you will. What was I thinking? If you can't find your way here, then you probably shouldn't be running operations at DCSS. It's 105 Stone Ridge Drive in Stonebriar Estates."

"Got it. I'll see you around six."

"Yes, six o'clock. Oh, wait. Did I give you my address already?"

"Yes, you did."

If I was reading the signs correctly, Ashley was a little excited.

◆ ◆ ◆ ◆

As I drove up the circle drive to 105 Stone Ridge Drive a little before six, I realized Ashley wasn't the only one feeling excited.

I was pretty pumped myself.

Other than my daughter, I hadn't gone out to eat with another woman since Emma passed away. Of course, I was only taking Ashley out to eat to fill her in on the details of our investigation.

This wasn't a date, nothing like that.

When I pulled the Lexus in front of her two-story white brick home with the professional-looking landscaping and the commercial grade security system, I caught myself shaking my head.

I felt sure DCSS had never employed an intern who lived in such an expensive neighborhood or in such luxurious surroundings, not to mention what was probably a million-dollar residence.

Ashley opened the door almost as soon as I rang the doorbell. "You found me? See? I knew you were good at your job."

I smiled. "I just looked for the house that had the most Christmas lights. I figured that was the one that belonged to you."

"How did you know I love Christmas lights?"

She gestured toward the living room where there was a gigantic tree in front of the windows with a zillion lights on it. "Would you believe I have a tree in every room?"

"Yes, I wouldn't have any problem believing that."

We both stood there in the foyer admiring the tree for a moment, and then she looked over at me and touched my arm. "Thanks for asking me to dinner, Silas. I'm really looking forward to hearing what Nixon told you, but I hope we don't have to spend the whole evening talking about the case. I've heard so many stories about you from my dad that I can't wait to find out if they're really true or not."

"I doubt if any of them are true, except maybe the one about me being a Dallas Cowboys fan. That one would be true."

She laughed and then pointed down the hallway in the direction of what I presumed was her kitchen. "Before we leave, I just need to go check on my babies. Would you like to come with me?"

"Uh . . . sure. I guess I . . . uh . . . didn't realize you had any kids."

She crooked her finger, and I followed her down the hallway.

◆ ◆ ◆ ◆

We walked through her kitchen, which looked like a gourmet chef's showpiece—stainless steel appliances, granite countertops, and distressed wood—and arrived in her laundry room.

Besides the washer and dryer and a bunch of cabinets, there was a large wooden crate along one wall.

The crate matched the finish on her cabinets.

"Silas, I'd like to introduce you to my babies."

Ashley gestured toward the crate where I could see a black standard poodle lying on a comfy-looking dog bed surrounded by five energetic puppies, all of whom were bouncing around like they had consumed too much caffeine.

"Oh, so these are your babies. Personally, I don't think the two-legged kind are nearly as cute as these four-legged ones."

"So you're a dog lover too? I thought that might be the case." She knelt down and stroked the mother's head. "This is Sissy, and she's one proud mama. Aren't you, Sissy? Aren't you proud?"

As if to answer her, Sissy began grooming one of her pups.

"Sure, I like dogs," I said, "but I couldn't say I was a dog lover. Since Marissa has allergies, we've never had a dog around the house."

"No need to worry about allergies with poodles. They don't shed, so most people don't have a problem with them."

As Ashley stood to her feet, one of the pups suddenly bolted from the crate and ran over to where I was standing.

"Oops," I said, "there's been a jailbreak." I knelt down and picked up the ball of curly black fur. "It looks like this little guy is tired of prison food." The pup immediately started licking my face, pressing his nose against my chest, and whining like I was about to abandon him at the orphanage.

"Uh-oh," Ashley said. "Watch out. I think you've been chosen."

As I stood there stroking the puppy's fur, I looked over at her and shook my head. "Wait a minute. What's going on here? Has Mike Norwell been talking to you? Did the two of you set this up?"

Ashley looked surprised. "What are you talking about? Mike and I didn't set anything up." She put her hands on her hips and glared at me. "Just what are you accusing me of?"

"I apologize. I didn't mean to sound accusatory. It's just that Mike's been nagging me about getting a dog, and he said when it was time for me to have one, the dog would find me. I think you can understand why I might be a little suspicious of this encounter."

Ashley smiled as she took the puppy from me. "Okay, now I get it, but he could be right, you know. All of my puppies are spoken for except for this little fella."

She held him up in front of me for a second.

"How about it? Could this little guy be yours?"

I stood there for a moment and looked at him.

Finally, I nodded. "You know. I believe he is. I think he's my guy."

As she put him back in the crate, she said, "Well, he'll have to stay with his mama a few more weeks, but he should be ready to go home with you in time for Christmas."

I chuckled. "I can't wait to hear what my daughter has to say about this. His arrival will certainly make for an interesting Christmas."

As we left the laundry room, Ashley asked, "Do you have any idea what you'll call him?"

"Didn't you hear me say his name already? He's my guy. I plan to call him Guy."

She laughed. "That's perfect. I bet you never imagined when you met me in the coffee shop on Monday that you'd be the proud owner of a dog named Guy by the end of the week."

"No, I can't say that I did."

I also never imagined I'd be looking forward to spending time with a woman, especially a woman like Ashley Davenport.

I wondered what other unexpected things were in my future.

Never The End, Always A Beginning

# ACKNOWLEDGEMENTS

Although many people have given me support and encouragement in the process of writing *One Wonders*, first and foremost, I want to thank my husband, James, and my daughter, Karis, who have never failed to uplift me with their prayers, strengthen me with their love, and bolster me with their confidence.

I also want to express a special word of gratitude to Lenda Selph and Kim Kemery, my incredible editor/proofers, and to all my beta readers, whose eye for detail continues to provide me with invaluable insight. You're the best!

And, to those experts out there who have given me advice, made suggestions, offered comments, and answered my questions, thank you! You know who you are, and I trust you know how much I appreciate you.

Last, but not least, I'm delighted to thank all my faithful readers. I hope you never stop asking, "When is your next book coming out?" You are my inspiration, and the reason I stay up writing past midnight.

# A NOTE TO MY READERS

Dear Reader,

Thank you for reading *One Wonders*, Book I in the Silas McKay Suspense Series. If you enjoyed it, you might also enjoy Book II, *Two Believe*, plus my other series, the Mylas Grey Mystery Series, featuring private investigator, Mylas Grey, and the Titus Ray Thriller Series, featuring CIA intelligence officer, Titus Ray, along with the spinoff of the series, *Ben in Love*, *Ben in Charge*, and *Ben in Trouble*, which are Titus Ray Thrillers featuring more of Ben Mitchell.

You'll find an excerpt from *Two Believe*, Book II in the Silas McKay Suspense Series, on the pages that follow. All my books are available in print, eBook, and audiobook exclusively on Amazon.

Would you do me a favor and post a review of *One Wonders* on Amazon? Since word-of-mouth testimonies and written reviews are usually the deciding factor in helping a reader pick out a book, they are an author's best friend and much appreciated!

Would you also consider signing up for my newsletter? You'll find a signup form on my website, **LuanaEhrlich.com**, where you'll be offered a FREE book in the Titus Ray Thriller Series just for signing up for my newsletter.

One of my greatest blessings comes from receiving email from my readers. My email address is **author@luanaehrlich.com.** I'd love to hear from you!

Excerpt from

**Two Believe**

*Book II in the Silas McKay Suspense Series*

# PART ONE

# Chapter 1

*Monday, December 5*

The last thing I wanted to do this Monday morning was drive an extra twenty minutes in Dallas rush hour traffic.

However, as I was leaving my house in Frisco and heading into my office at Mockingbird Lane and Preston Road, I got a call from Austin Tomlin asking me to meet him at the Metro Market Center in downtown Dallas, and I immediately agreed to do it.

I said yes primarily because Tomlin was my boss.

Of course, I was also curious why he wanted to meet me in the parking lot of the prestigious marketing establishment, but I figured it had something to do with DCSS, the security agency Tomlin owned, and where I had the responsibility of running operations, a position I took five years ago.

DCSS, or Discreet Corporate Security Services, provided a wide range of security assistance for mid-size businesses and large corporations, including assessing employee problems, identifying operational mismanagement, analyzing intellectual property theft, and investigating suspected fraud and other misconduct.

Although Tomlin usually stayed out of the day-to-day operations of DCSS—he paid me the big bucks to do that—he occasionally asked me to go with him to meet a new client, and I wondered if that was what was happening at the Metro Market Center today.

Tomlin didn't ask if it was a convenient time for me to meet him.

However, that didn't surprise me.

Tomlin spent twenty-five years in the Army before he retired and started his second career, so giving orders was second nature to him.

By the same token, I'd spent eight years in the Defense Intelligence Agency as a covert operative, so I was used to taking them.

That didn't mean I didn't ask him a few questions, though.

"Do we have a new client at the Metro Market Center?"

"That's correct. I got an emergency call from Phillip Shaheen about an hour ago."

"I'm sorry, Austin, but that name doesn't ring a bell with me. Who's Phillip Shaheen?"

"I thought perhaps you knew Phillip. He's the owner of Gadise Diamonds, the jewelry store in the Market Center. I don't know what his problem is, but we'll find out in a few minutes. I'm pulling into the east parking lot at the Market Center now. You'll find me in Row F."

With that, Tomlin hung up.

Although I'd heard of Gadise Diamonds, I had no idea who actually owned the company, but Tomlin's familiarity with the owner of the upscale jewelry store was something I'd come to expect from him.

Tomlin had hundreds of friends.

Whether it was because of his years at DCSS, his contacts in the military, or the fact he'd recently been hired as a security analyst on a cable news network, I wasn't sure why he knew so many people.

Even so, since DCSS mostly catered to large corporations, it seemed strange the jewelry store owner had gotten in touch with Tomlin.

Ordinarily, before I met with a new client, I learned as much as I could about the company before I actually met the client in person. Obviously, in this case, that was impossible, but I figured if anyone might know something about Gadise Diamonds, it would be my administrative assistant, Claudia Hensley, so I gave her a call.

"Good morning, Claudia. I'm meeting Austin at the Metro Market Center about a new client, so I wanted to let you know I won't be in the office until later this morning."

"That's fine. You don't have any appointments until later."

"That would be my two o'clock staff meeting, right?"

"That's right. There's nothing else on your schedule, and the only item I have on the agenda for the meeting is closing the case on Victor Perry and Falcon Aeronautics. By the way, who's the new client?"

"Gadise Diamonds. At least, I think the jewelry store is the new client. Austin didn't exactly spell that out for me. I suppose it could be the owner himself. Austin also mentioned him."

"Oh, wow. Gadise Diamonds. That's an impressive jewelry store."

"I figured that might get your attention. Have you ever shopped there before?"

"Just once, and it was only to look around. I already knew I couldn't afford anything before I ever stepped foot in the door."

"High-dollar stuff, right? Otherwise, how could they afford a store in that location?"

"Yes, it's pricey but also high quality. It doesn't sound like you've ever been there before, but I can't believe you never purchased Emma a little trinket from Gadise Diamonds for some special occasion."

Claudia was the only person at DCSS who wasn't tentative about bringing up my late wife's name in a conversation.

My wife Emma died of a brain tumor six months ago, and most of my colleagues were still tiptoeing around it, acting embarrassed, or looking concerned every time her name came up.

Claudia, on the other hand, was more of a "tough love" kind of person, so I suspected she thought bringing up Emma's name every chance she got was the best way for me to deal with my grief.

"No, I've never been to Gadise Diamonds before, and I doubt if Emma would have wanted a gift from there. She was more of a practical person, as I'm sure you remember."

"Yes, I remember, but even a practical woman loves diamonds. I can testify to that myself."

"In that case, would you mind doing some research for me on the jewelry store? Austin knows the owner, but he may not know anything about the business."

"No, I don't mind. I'll see what I can find out about it. I'll probably have it for you by the time you get here."

"Okay, thanks, Claudia. I'll see you in a couple of hours."

"Should I also let Ashley Davenport know about the staff meeting?"

"Yes, even though she's an intern, I'd like to have her there. She was with me at Victor Perry's house when we ended up calling the police, so the rest of the staff may want to ask her some questions."

"Buck stopped by my office this morning and gave me the details about Victor, but I'll wait to hear the story from you before I put anything in the files. You know how Buck tends to exaggerate stuff."

Buck Greiner was the head of the Surveillance Division at DCSS, and although Claudia was right—he *did* like to embellish things a little—I couldn't ask for a better surveillance guy.

"Well, yeah, he does like to add some color, but if Buck told you the situation got a little dicey, he wasn't exaggerating."

"Actually, the whole thing sounded pretty dangerous. I expect Ashley thought so too."

I couldn't tell whether she was hinting for more information about Ashley or more information about the Victor Perry case, but I told her I'd fill her in on everything later and hung up.

That wasn't exactly true, though.

I wasn't about to fill her in on everything about Ashley Davenport.

◆ ◆ ◆ ◆

Ashley was a new intern at DCSS—Tomlin hired about a dozen each year—but she wasn't one of our typical interns.

Ordinarily, the interns at DCSS were fresh out of college.

Some of them were waiting to get into the police academy, while others were still trying to make up their mind about what they wanted to do with their degrees in criminal justice. A few were recent graduates of the Professional Investigators Academy at the University of North Texas and were hoping their internship with DCSS would eventually lead to a permanent position with us.

Ashley wasn't fresh out of college.

After receiving her business degree at SMU, she stuck around and got her master's in business management. After that, she traveled around Europe for a couple of years before finally coming back to Dallas and working for her dad before deciding she wanted to become a private detective.

Even though Ashley had a graduate degree from SMU, she still went through the PI Academy at North Texas. However, unlike other students who came to us from the Academy, she wasn't hoping to get a permanent position with DCSS after her internship.

Ashley didn't plan to go to work for anyone after her internship. She planned to start her own detective agency.

She even had a name for it—Precept Detective Agency—and her father, Duncan Davenport, was bankrolling the whole thing.

Duncan was the CEO of Precept Healthcare, our highest-paying corporate client at DCSS, and he was the reason Tomlin agreed to allow Ashley to do an internship with us in the first place.

Those circumstances played a major role in the decision I made to mentor Ashley when she asked me if I'd be willing to do so after Buck introduced us last week.

When she said her father specifically told her she should approach me about showing her the ropes at DCSS, I didn't feel I could say no, even though I wanted to turn her down as soon as she brought it up.

Not that I had anything against Ashley personally.

I just didn't want to spend time with another woman so soon after Emma's death, especially a woman only four years younger than me.

To make it easy on myself, I decided to have Ashley help me with the Victor Perry case. It seemed like an ideal situation because I didn't think it would take that long to figure out if Perry was selling Falcon Aeronautics proprietary information to a competitor.

I was right about that. It didn't take that long.

On the other hand, I was wrong about Ashley.

I discovered I didn't mind spending time with her.

I wasn't sure what to make of that.

◆ ◆ ◆ ◆

I immediately put Ashley Davenport out of my mind as I pulled my black Lexus in the east parking lot at the Metro Market Center and drove over to Row F, where I found Tomlin's silver Audi A7.

He was sitting behind the wheel drinking from a commuter cup—the same color as his vehicle—while talking on his cell phone.

I tapped on the window a couple of times, and he clicked the lock on the passenger-side door. As I slid in the seat, Tomlin told his caller goodbye.

"Hi, Silas," he said. "I was just talking to Phillip Shaheen. He's in the store right now," he inclined his head toward the multi-story Market Center building in front of us, "so I told him we'd be dropping in on him in a few minutes."

"Okay. I'm anxious to hear what this is about."

He raised his cup to his lips—I assumed it was coffee since I seldom saw him without a cup—but then he lowered it a moment later and said, "Do you need some coffee? We can stop inside and get you some, if you like. I'm sorry I didn't think to bring you a cup."

"No, I'm good. I had plenty before I left home."

"Honestly, I don't know what Phillip needs from us. When he called me this morning, he said he had an emergency at his store which required the utmost discretion. He said he felt sure DCSS would be able to help him."

"How do the two of you know each other?"

He chuckled. "We met in the Green Room at the KEFW studio when we were both being interviewed for the Dante Garmond Show—on separate topics, of course. I believe Garmond interviewed Phillip about a huge diamond recently found in Botswana, and I was there answering questions about the scandal you uncovered at the Morosoi biotechnical firm. Remember that one? Their employee was caught selling trade secrets to a Chinese pharmaceutical company."

"I won't soon forget that one, but it's hard to believe Phillip's emergency has anything to do with stolen intellectual property."

"No, I doubt if that's the case. It could even be personal, but since he said he wanted DCSS to investigate something, I told him I'd be bringing my operations director with me. I figured you were available since you were able to close the Falcon Aeronautics case on Friday."

"Yes, we had a fast turnaround on that one."

"Ashley Davenport was with you, wasn't she? I played golf with Duncan on Saturday, and he was very pleased to hear you had agreed to mentor his daughter. We're in negotiations for him to sign another five-year contract with us, so I was glad to hear that."

"She handled herself very well; much better than I anticipated."

Before Tomlin could reply, the screen on his cell phone lit up with a text message, and once he glanced down at it, he said, "This is a text from Beverly. I asked her to get me some facts about Gadise

Diamonds."

Beverly Sanger was Tomlin's administrative assistant. If she ever retired, I imagine Tomlin would do so as well.

"She says Gadise Diamonds leases a permanent showroom on the fourth floor of the Market Center. They have around three thousand square feet, and Beverly estimates their lease is around a hundred thousand a year. They've been there for the past twenty-five years."

"That's a hefty lease. They must be making quite a profit."

"I'm sure that's true. I know they only carry high-end pieces. I bought Wynona a necklace from there for a gala we attended, and it cost me more than her dress."

I didn't have any trouble believing that. Whenever I'd been around Austin's wife, Wynona, she always looked as if she could have just stepped off the pages of a fashion magazine.

I gestured at his phone. "I don't suppose Beverly sent you anything about Phillip Shaheen, did she?"

He slipped his phone back in his jacket pocket. "No, but Phillip didn't seem to mind talking about himself when I met him, so feel free to ask him any questions. In fact, I encourage you to do that. I'm sure he'll be expecting your questions."

"Why is that?"

He smiled. "Because I told him your specialty was asking a lot of questions."

I shrugged. "That's because I'm always looking for answers."

"Exactly, and that's what Phillip said he needed."

# Chapter 2

The Metro Market Center was a fifteen-story concrete structure surrounding an open atrium with glass-enclosed elevators in the center of the building. Colorful flags from every nation around the world were hanging from the balconies of each of the floors.

I'd been in the Market Center a couple of times, and each time I'd never failed to be impressed by how affluent the place looked.

It looked like money. It sounded like money—unidentifiable music was playing in the background—and it even smelled like money.

Of course, that scent was probably due to the perfumed air being pumped through the ventilation system, a service that used to be reserved for the finest hotels and was now being offered to retail establishments.

I tried to identify the fragrance after the doors on the middle elevator whooshed shut and Tomlin and I began our ascent to the fourth floor, but the only thing that came to mind was a combination of chocolate and lavender with perhaps a hint of leather.

Whatever it was, it was a very pleasant scent.

We shared the elevator with two older ladies who ignored our presence as they discussed the Christmas gifts they were about to purchase for their spouses at an exclusive men's store located next door to Gadise Diamonds.

However, I noticed when they came out of the elevator and headed toward the men's clothing store, they paused to look in the Gadise Diamonds display window.

Their noses were pressed up to the glass as we went inside.

We were met by a blonde woman wearing a black jacket with the Gadise Diamonds logo—gold, silver, and black bars shaped like a diamond—on the left front pocket.

"Good morning, Gentlemen. How may I assist you today?"

Tomlin said, "We're here to meet with Mr. Shaheen. I'm Austin Tomlin, and this is Silas McKay. Mr. Shaheen is expecting us."

"Of course. Please wait here a moment."

While we waited for her to return, I assessed their security setup and memorized the layout of the store.

The store's color scheme was black, gold, and silver in keeping with the brand's logo. Thus, the carpet was light gray, the display cases were black and gold, and the walls were metallic silver. The chandeliers—there were five of them—appeared to be crystal.

The store was wide, rather than deep, and I didn't see any sales terminals anywhere. Evidently, a customer was taken to a separate room to pay for a purchase.

I observed this taking place when a young couple followed a male clerk over towards the back of the store where there were three closed doors with a sign on each one that said, "Transactions."

When the clerk opened one of the doors and ushered the couple inside, I caught a brief glimpse of the décor—a black granite-topped table surrounded by gold leather chairs.

As he closed the door, my attention immediately shifted to a middle-aged man wearing a gray suit, black tie, and black loafers who was smiling as he made his way toward us.

"Austin," he said, offering Tomlin his hand, "it's wonderful to see you again. Thanks for coming by."

After the two men shook hands, Tomlin looked at me and said, "Phillip, I'd like you to meet my operations director, Silas McKay. Silas, this is Phillip Shaheen. He owns this incredible store."

Once we were finished with the social niceties, Shaheen invited us to his office, which was through a set of double doors on the east side of the store and down a short hallway. As we made our way down the hallway, I noticed three other offices besides Shaheen's, as well as a security console with several closed-circuit television monitors.

I nodded at the security guard seated behind the console, and he gave me a quick two-fingered salute.

As we walked inside Shaheen's office, he motioned at the chairs in front of his desk and invited Tomlin and me to be seated.

While his office had the same color scheme and luxurious vibe as the store itself, it was cluttered with stacks of catalogs and various kinds of jewelry boxes bearing the Gadise logo. Most of these items were piled on a credenza behind his desk. On the desk itself was a collection of large, well-used black notebooks.

Shaheen pushed a couple of the notebooks aside as he sat down.

"I really appreciate your coming by on such short notice, Austin. I would have made an appointment at your office, but since this is where the theft took place, I thought it might be better if we met here."

"I was happy to come by, Phillip. So are you saying the emergency you mentioned is a robbery?"

He waffled his hand back and forth. "I wouldn't really call it a robbery since we didn't have a break-in and no one was held at gunpoint, but I did have something stolen. It was a man's signet ring worth $65,000. It disappeared from our store on Saturday."

"What do you mean by disappeared?" I asked.

Shaheen laid both hands on top of his desk as if he might be trying to calm himself and said, "I mean the ring was shown to a customer, along with several other rings, and when the customer left the store thirty minutes later, the ring was gone."

"I noticed you have security cameras throughout your store," I said. "What did they show?"

"Unfortunately, they didn't show him taking the ring, but that's what my sales associate believes happened, and I'm inclined to believe him because I know the identity of the customer, and that's part of the problem."

I noticed Tomlin shifting his weight in his chair, so I figured he was probably getting frustrated at the piecemeal way Shaheen was explaining the problem, or maybe my boss was just upset at himself for agreeing to help Shaheen when the man's problem sounded more like a petty theft situation—albeit a $65,000 petty theft.

Tomlin wasn't in the habit of accepting such cases.

He was adamant about DCSS staying true to its name and only dealing with large corporations or high-profile cases.

I said, "In order for us to understand what happened on Saturday, would you mind starting at the beginning when the customer entered your store and take us step-by-step through what transpired?"

"That's a good idea," Tomlin said. "Is this person a regular customer? Is that why you know him?"

Shaheen sat back in his chair and sighed. "No, he's not a regular customer, but he's been in the store several times. And yes, I know him. His name is Todd Harriman, and he usually comes in with his father, Danny Harriman. Are you familiar with that name?"

"Surely you're not talking about the owner of the Metro Market Center," Tomlin said. "You don't mean *that* Danny Harriman."

"Yes, and I understand why you're surprised. The man is a billionaire, so why would his son steal a ring from me when he could probably afford to buy it outright with his weekly allowance."

"You've got to admit it sounds pretty far-fetched," Tomlin said.

"Oh, I admit that, but after speaking to my sales associates and viewing the security tape, I haven't been able to come up with any other explanation for what happened. Unfortunately, I wasn't on the floor at the time, although I *was* here in my office."

"I suppose we'll be able to view the security video for ourselves as well as speak to your employees?" Tomlin asked.

"Of course. Melvin Williams is the sales associate who assisted Todd when he came in the store on Saturday. According to him, Todd came in shortly after ten o'clock and asked to see our men's signet rings. When Melvin inquired about whether Todd wanted a monogram, a gemstone, or perhaps a coat of arms, he immediately said he wanted a diamond signet ring."

"Signet rings were used to seal documents in the Middle Ages, weren't they?" I asked. "I've never pictured them having diamonds."

"You're right. Signet rings were designed with the family crest, but now they're made with gemstones, initials, symbols, or whatever the person wants. I'm sure you've seen Super Bowl rings before. Those rings are just signet rings, although they're extra large and have a substantial number of diamonds on them."

"And Todd wanted a diamond signet ring," Tomlin said. "I suppose that would be the most expensive kind of signet ring?"

"Most definitely," Shaheen said, nodding his head as he reached over and flipped open one of the black notebooks in front of him. "Here, I'll show you."

Shaheen put on a pair of glasses and pointed to a two-page spread of diamond signet rings. Tomlin and I both leaned forward and looked at them as he turned the notebook towards us.

I admit I wasn't looking so much at the design of the rings as the prices underneath them. The rings ranged anywhere from $5,000 to $25,000.

"Were these the type of rings Todd was shown?" I asked.

"At the beginning, yes. These rings are one to two carats, depending on the cut of the diamonds, but after Todd looked them over, he asked Melvin to see something in the two to three carat range, and that's when he brought out the $65,000 ring, along with several others."

"How many rings did he show Todd?" I asked.

"By the time he brought out the most expensive rings, there were eighteen rings on display on three separate trays on the counter."

Shaheen opened a cabinet behind him and pulled out three black leather jewelry display trays lined in black velvet. Each one looked to be about fourteen inches long and ten inches wide.

"At Gadise Diamonds, our sales associates are trained to present each ring to the customer separately. You'll clearly be able to see that on the security camera video. What Melvin did was place a ring insert in each tray, and then he added a ring to the insert while he was describing the ring's features to Todd."

We watched as Shaheen reached behind him and selected a black velvet ring insert with slots for eight rings. After placing it in the display tray, he said, "This is how the tray and insert appeared on the counter, and this is how it looked with a ring in it."

He removed a black onyx ring from his pinky finger and placed it in the ring insert. "Something like this."

"You said there were three trays on display. Can I assume there was a ring insert in each tray?" I asked.

Shaheen nodded, "That's correct."

"If your sales associate showed Todd eighteen rings in all, then there had to be some empty slots in the ring inserts. Otherwise, there would have been twenty-four rings on display."

"There *were* some empty slots. That's true. Perhaps that's why Melvin didn't immediately notice the ring was missing until after Todd left the store. If I remember correctly, one tray had six rings on display, one had seven, and the last one had five. The last tray held the most expensive rings."

"How long has your sales associate been with you?" Tomlin asked.

"Melvin?" Shaheen looked off in the distance. "Hmmm. Let's see. I'd say about fifteen years."

"Have you ever questioned his honesty?"

"Oh my, no. Of course not. If you're implying he could have taken the ring, that's something I could never imagine. He's been handling jewelry here at Gadise Diamonds for a long time."

I said, "In-house thefts are usually crimes of opportunity. The thief doesn't necessarily have the mindset of a criminal."

Shaheen extended his palms toward me. "By all means, Silas, feel free to question Melvin. You have my permission to do so."

Tomlin said, "We may have gotten a little ahead of ourselves here, Phillip. Why do you want DCSS to look into this matter for you? Don't you think the Dallas Police can handle it for you?"

"They probably could, but I haven't told the police about the missing ring. I don't want to involve the DPD in this matter. That's why I called you. When I asked you about the kind of services your agency provided, you mentioned your clientele were companies who required the utmost discretion when it came to investigating criminal activity. That's what I need here, discretion."

"You mean because you suspect the ring was stolen by Todd Harriman, and you lease this space from his father?" Tomlin asked. "Is that why you want us to look into this for you?"

"Yes. Do you blame me? The waiting list for retailers who want to lease space here is a mile long. It's the most coveted location in downtown Dallas. If I were to accuse his son of stealing from me, Danny Harriman would kick me out of here before Christmas."

Tomlin was quiet for a moment.

A few seconds later, he nodded. "I hear you. It's a delicate situation." After another pause, he slapped both hands on his knees and said, "Okay, Phillip, we'll take your case as long as you understand you're required to sign a contract with DCSS, and our services don't come cheap."

"I'm not concerned about the cost, and I'm happy to sign a contract with you. Do you want to fax it to me or just email it?"

"I'll have my administrative assistant take care of that as soon as I get back to the office."

Tomlin stood to his feet and gestured at me. "And now, I'll leave you in the very capable hands of Silas. Otherwise, I won't be able to make it to my ten-thirty appointment in time."

Shaheen stood up and offered Tomlin his hand. "Thank you, Austin. I really appreciate your help with this." He gestured at the door. "Here, I'll walk you out."

After they shook hands, Tomlin said, "There's no need to do that, Phillip. You stay here and answer Silas's questions. I assure you he has a bunch of them for you."

Once Tomlin closed the door behind him, Shaheen sat down at his desk again and gestured at me. "I'm happy to answer whatever questions you may have, Silas, but besides showing you the security video, I really think I've told you everything."

"No, not quite everything."

"What am I missing?"

"You haven't explained why Todd stole the ring from you."

He stared at me. "How would I know that?"

"You mentioned you knew Todd. The way you phrased that led me to believe it was more than just a passing acquaintance. It sounded personal to me."

He steepled both hands together under his chin and nodded. "Okay, you're right. There *is* a personal element to my relationship to Todd, and it's partly the reason I suspect he's the person who stole the ring. I didn't mention it because I didn't want to prejudice you."

"It won't prejudice me. Tell me about that personal element."

# Chapter 3

Before Shaheen explained what he meant by the personal element to his story, he offered me some coffee, and when I accepted, he picked up his phone and asked the person on the other end of the line to bring us some.

While we waited for it to arrive, he cleared a spot on his desk and a few minutes later, a woman wearing a black dress walked in his office and set a tray down in that spot.

The tray held a carafe along with two white bone china cups and matching saucers. The cups were rimmed in silver and written on the side in gold script was Gadise Diamonds. Beneath it was their logo.

The woman—Shaheen never introduced her—poured us each a cup of coffee, and after she asked me if I wanted cream or sugar—I didn't—she set the cup and saucer in front of me and left the room.

"Can I assume your VIP customers are treated to this kind of service when they shop here?" I asked.

He smiled. "Yes. We have two private lounges on the east side of our showroom where our VIP customers receive our exclusive pampered treatment. Of course, I won't give out any names, but our VIP customers include movie celebrities, sport stars, television personalities, and political figures, among many others."

"I'm guessing your sales associate didn't give Todd Harriman the VIP treatment when he was in the store on Saturday."

His smile turned to a frown. "No, and when I tell you why he didn't, you'll understand what I meant by the personal element in this theft."

I only made a few comments as Shaheen told me about a Christmas party he attended last year with his wife and daughter at the Harriman estate—his description of Danny Harriman's residence.

"Danny has an elegant Christmas party every year for his tenants here at the Market Center. He calls it the Harriman Christmas Gala. It's a formal affair, held at his estate, and all the tenants are issued extra invitations so their family members can attend."

"Do you attend every year?"

"Yes, but it was the first time my daughter, Lela, ever attended the gala. Previously, she was too young or she was away at college. However, when she graduated from Cornell University in May, she took a position with an investment firm here in Dallas, so she was excited about finally being able to attend the Gala."

Shaheen said as soon as he arrived with his wife and daughter, Todd Harriman took an immediate interest in Lela, and they ended up spending most of the evening together. However, Shaheen wasn't too happy with all the charm Todd showered on Lela because he'd heard he was a playboy, and he collected beautiful women like trophies.

When Shaheen paused and took a drink of his coffee, I was tempted to ask him how Lela responded to the attention Todd gave her, but I decided to let him finish.

"Following the party, Todd took Lela out to dinner a couple of times, and I suppose he knew about my feelings, because Lela said he asked her why I didn't approve of him. Well, in the end, Lela dumped him, so I thought that would be the end of the story."

After drinking the last of my coffee, I put my cup back on the saucer and pushed it aside, but when Shaheen noticed it was empty, he gestured at the carafe and invited me to have another cup.

"No thanks," I said, "but that was excellent coffee. So tell me, why wasn't that the end of the story? What happened?"

"The next time I stopped by Danny's office suite to speak to the Market Center's maintenance engineer, I ran into Todd. I greeted him pleasantly enough, but he immediately got up in my face and asked me why I'd forbidden my daughter to date him. Even though I insisted I'd done no such thing, he didn't believe me. When he walked away, he said, 'I promise you, you'll live to regret that decision.'"

"When did that encounter take place?"

"Several months ago. I think it was back in March, but he's continued to give me the cold shoulder when he comes by the store with his father. Danny pays a courtesy call on his tenants every two to three months, and when that happens, Todd usually wanders around the store and doesn't enter into the conversation I'm having with his father, although he used to do that sort of thing."

"Does Todd work for his father?"

"Yes, he's in charge of advertising for the Market Center, and I've noticed his ads for the past six months haven't included Gadise Diamonds. Since the store is so well-known, it hasn't hurt us, but I was beginning to wonder if that's what he meant about regretting my decision. Now, I believe he's taken it a step further."

"You mean by stealing the expensive ring?"

He nodded. "I'm sure he knows if I accuse him of taking the ring, his father will believe him instead of me, especially if I don't have any proof to back it up. The timing is also a little suspect because my lease renews in January, and if I were to implicate Todd in the theft, there's a good chance Danny would refuse to renew my lease."

"You really think Todd planned it out that carefully?"

"Yes, I do, and I suspect he was aware of how our security cameras were positioned before he ever asked to see the rings. That's why it's impossible to tell in the video when he actually takes the ring."

"If you don't mind, I'd like to take a look at that video now."

"Sure. I'll have our security officer come in and show it to you. His name is Wes Shelton. There are actually several videos to look at."

"Would I be able to take a copy of them with me so our people at DCSS can take a look at them too?"

"That shouldn't be a problem." He picked up his phone. "I'll have Wes put everything on a flash drive for you."

While he was giving his security guy some instructions, I studied the photographs of the diamond signet rings in the black notebook. Once he hung up, I asked, "Do you have a photograph of the actual ring that was stolen?"

"Yes," he said, reaching over and picking up a manila envelope, "I have it right here, along with the ring's description and certification."

When I took the envelope from him, I noticed it already had our company's name, Discreet Corporate Security Services, written across the front with Tomlin's name below that.

I pointed to the writing on the envelope and said, "It looks like you were pretty sure Austin would agree to take your case or was that just wishful thinking on your part?"

Shaheen let out a short laugh. "I can understand why you're the Head of Operations at DCSS, Silas. You don't miss a thing, do you?"

I gave him a smile but didn't say anything.

I hoped he would get the hint and answer my question.

He nodded. "Yes, I was fairly certain Austin would take the case. When I met him in the Green Room at the KEFW studio, he mentioned DCSS specialized in corporate espionage, but he said he occasionally took cases involving high-profile businessmen, so I was counting on him taking this case."

I didn't ask whether he considered himself the high-profile businessman, or whether he was referring to Danny Harriman.

However, knowing Tomlin, I figured he took the case because it involved Harriman.

My boss was intrigued by billionaires.

I was intrigued by the possibility a billionaire's son stole a diamond ring from a jewelry store in broad daylight.

◆ ◆ ◆ ◆

A few seconds later, there was a knock on Shaheen's door, and his security officer, Wes Shelton—the guy I'd seen in the hallway monitoring the cameras at the security console—came in the room carrying a laptop.

Once he made the introductions, Shaheen said, "I need to go see how things are going out on the showroom floor, so I'll let you and Wes look at the security videos by yourself. I'll probably be back here before you're finished."

After Shaheen left, Wes sat down in the chair recently occupied by Tomlin and placed his laptop on the desk. "Mr. Shaheen is a little paranoid about keeping an eye on the store since the ring was stolen."

"Has the store ever been robbed before?"

"Not since I've been here, and that's been eight years." He shook his head. "I'm really sorry it happened on my watch. I understand you work for an agency that specializes in security, so maybe you'll see something on these videos that I didn't see."

Wes raised the lid on his laptop and pulled up a diagram of the store's floorplan, pointing out where the cameras were positioned around the store.

After I studied the diagram a few minutes, he clicked on a software program that displayed six screens side-by-side where the view from each of the cameras on the floor of the showroom could be seen.

On the laptop, the screens were positioned three across in two rows, and I was able to clearly see Phillip Shaheen in the middle screen chatting with a customer on the showroom floor.

A few seconds later, Wes clicked on a couple of tabs and brought up the archived videos from Saturday. The timestamp at the bottom of the screen showed 10:06.

"This starts a few seconds before Todd Harriman entered the store on Saturday morning," Wes said.

"Would I be able to see what was happening before Todd showed up? Could you show me the feed starting at around nine forty-five?"

"Oh, sure. No problem."

After he clicked on another tab, I observed where each sales associate and customer was located on the floor of the showroom at Gadise Diamonds before Todd entered the store.

Wes identified each associate for me, and as he was doing so, I pulled out my cell phone and wrote down their names in an encrypted note-taking application developed by my deputy, Mike Norwell.

There were four sales associates. Two were helping customers and two were positioned at opposite ends of the store arranging displays. The clerk nearest the door was Melvin, who ended up helping Todd.

Of the two associates helping customers, one was a male associate assisting a young couple with some wedding rings, and the other was a female associate showing some diamond bracelets to a woman. The woman was all by herself and was pregnant. She was so large, she looked like she could have her baby at any time.

After putting away my cell phone, I said, "Thanks, Wes. I believe I'm ready to see what happens when Todd shows up."

He nodded and clicked on the video that began at 10:06.

◆ ◆ ◆ ◆

When Todd Harriman walked into Gadise Diamonds, he paused a few seconds in the doorway and looked around the showroom, moving his head from left to right.

He was dressed in a brown sports jacket, open-collar shirt, and brown dress pants. His thick blond hair was longer on top than it was on the sides, and he was clean-shaven.

I thought his eyes looked blue, but I couldn't tell for sure. Whether his eyes were blue or green, he was a good-looking guy, and despite the quality of the video, it was easy to tell he had a lot of self-confidence about him. I figured he was in his late thirties.

Melvin, the sales associate who was standing nearest the door, looked up from the display case he'd been arranging.

When he smiled at Todd, I was pretty sure he recognized him.

There was no sound with the video, but since Shaheen had already told us what went on, it was easy to understand what happened after the two men spoke for a few minutes, and why Melvin directed Todd over to a counter where the signet rings were on display.

As Melvin took each ring out of the display case and placed it in a ring holder on the black velvet display tray, he appeared to be describing the various attributes of each one.

However, from the profile I could see of Todd's face—he was standing at an angle to the camera—it was obvious he wasn't interested in these particular rings.

In fact, he never tried them on or touched them in any way.

Melvin spoke with him a few minutes, nodding his head as if he were in complete agreement with whatever Todd was saying, and then he turned to the display case behind him and removed a few more rings—presumably, the high-dollar rings.

At this point, Todd positioned himself directly in front of Melvin, and his profile could no longer be seen on the security camera.

All I could see was Todd's back, although occasionally, I could see his hands when he tried on one of the rings and held it up in front of him, admiring the way it looked on his finger.

He did this three different times.

Melvin, like any good salesperson, stopped talking to Todd and allowed the product to speak for itself when that happened.

Since Melvin's face was the only one I could see, I studied it to get an idea of what Todd might be saying to him.

The third time Todd held his hand up to admire the ring on his finger, I saw a concerned look come over Melvin's face.

However, his attention wasn't directed at Todd.

He was looking at something across the room.

I quickly glanced at another camera view of the showroom and noticed the female sales associate who'd been showing the pregnant woman the diamond bracelets had her arm around the mother-to-be and was helping her over to a bench.

At the same time, another sales associate was rushing over to her side with some bottled water and offering it to her. The pregnant lady gave him a weak smile and took the water from him.

To Melvin's credit, he remained at his spot in front of Todd and didn't hurry over to offer to help them, which would have left the three trays of diamond rings out in the open and vulnerable to anyone who walked in the store—as well as to his customer.

Todd didn't appear to know what was going on behind him.

He never even turned around.

A few minutes later, Todd shook his head at Melvin, gave him a wave, and walked out the front door.

After Todd left, Melvin gestured toward the associates helping the pregnant woman and seemed to be asking if he could be of any assistance. At that point, the woman stood to her feet, gave the saleslady who'd been helping her a hug, picked up her purse from the counter, and left the store.

My attention switched back to Melvin as he began putting away the signet rings he'd been showing Todd. He took his time doing it, examining each ring and then using a polish cloth to wipe away any smudges before returning it to the display case.

When he got to the third tray, his eyes immediately got big.

He froze for a few seconds.

Moments later, he bent down and started looking all around the area where he'd been standing.

When he came up empty-handed, he pulled out the jewelry trays he'd just returned to the display case and examined each one again.

By this time, Melvin looked flushed, and there was an expression of panic on his face.

After locking the display case, he walked over and opened the door that led to the hallway outside Shaheen's office, briefly disappearing from view for a moment.

When he reappeared, Wes was with him.

"You can stop the recording now," I told Wes, who'd been watching the whole thing with me.

"Well, what do you think?" he asked, tapping his finger on the computer's touchpad to freeze the video. "Are you able to tell what happened to the ring?"

"No, not in this first viewing, but I'm anxious to have some of my people at DCSS take a look at it."

He reached in his pocket and pulled out a flash drive. "Here's a copy for you to take with you."

"Thanks," I said, slipping it inside my jacket. "If you don't mind, I'd like to ask you some questions now."

"Sure. Fire away."

"Are you the person responsible for positioning the cameras around the store?"

# Chapter 4

Wes hesitated for a moment, and then he slowly nodded his head, but as he was about to say something, the door opened and Phillip Shaheen walked in.

"Were you able to see the video?" he asked, pointing at the laptop.

"Yes, we just finished."

"Any first impressions?"

"Like I told Wes, I didn't see what happened to the ring, but that was mainly because Todd had his back to the camera. Naturally, I'm curious about the positioning of the security cameras, since some of the cameras only show a view of the sales associates and not the customers."

"That's the way Phillip said the cameras should be set up, and I agreed with him," Wes said, looking over at Shaheen as if seeking his approval. "Since the cameras are there to record what's happening with both the customers and the sales associates, we decided some of them should be pointed in one direction and some in the other."

"Personally, I believe that's why Todd asked to see the diamond signet rings," Shaheen said. "He had been in the store enough to observe where the cameras were positioned, so he must have realized if he stood at that particular spot, his actions couldn't be recorded."

"Are the cameras ever changed?" I asked. "Do you have them turned in one direction for a certain period of time and then randomly reposition them without notifying your employees?"

Wes shook his head. "No, but maybe we should do that."

After Shaheen agreed with him, I looked down at the names of the sales associates on my phone and said, "I don't have time today to interview everyone who was on the floor when the ring was taken, but if he's available now, I'd like to speak to Melvin Williams."

Shaheen said, "Yes, Melvin's working today. I'll go ask him to join you in one of our VIP lounges so the two of you can talk privately. It shouldn't take me but a couple of minutes to make the arrangements."

Wes closed the lid on his laptop and started to follow Shaheen out the door, but then I realized I needed to ask him something else.

"Wes, I have another question for you."

He paused at the door. "Oh, sure. What is it?"

"What did Melvin say to you when he came out of the showroom and told you the ring was missing?"

He looked up at the ceiling a few seconds. "Ah . . . let's see . . . I believe he asked me if I saw what happened. Yes, that's it. He was very excited, and I didn't understand him at first. I actually thought he meant did I see the pregnant woman who was feeling dizzy."

"Is that what was wrong with her?"

"Yes, that's what Elizabeth told me later. Elizabeth is the sales associate who was helping her with the diamond bracelets. She said the pregnant lady told her she needed to sit down because she was feeling light-headed."

"When you realized Melvin wasn't talking about the pregnant lady, but instead he was asking you if you saw what happened when he was showing Todd the rings, what did you say?"

"I told him I hadn't seen anything. That's when he informed me he was missing one of the rings he'd been showing Todd Harriman. Once he said that, I went out to the showroom to help him look for it. I thought he might have dropped it on the floor. It was only later that we realized Todd must have taken it." He shook his head. "I didn't envy Melvin having to tell Phillip about the ring, that's for sure."

"I suppose you already knew who Todd was?"

"Oh, yes. I recognized him when he came in."

"How would you describe his behavior?"

"Well, I guess I'd say it was normal for him. He's always seemed arrogant, like he was above it all. His father isn't like that, though."

"When Todd visited the store with his father, did you get the feeling he was checking out the security, looking at where the cameras were located, anything like that?"

He shook his head. "Not really, and I'm always watching for that sort of behavior with all our customers, but I'm sure I wasn't as alert with him as I am with customers I don't know. Truthfully, Todd is the last person I would expect to steal from this store."

"So you think he took the ring?"

He motioned at the laptop in his hand. "I know you didn't see the rest of the video of what happened when Melvin came and got me, but when you watch it, you'll be able to see how the two of us covered every inch of that area by the display counters. That ring didn't drop on the floor. It had to be in Todd's pocket when he walked out."

"When do you think he slipped it in there?"

"Melvin can probably answer that better than me, but from viewing the video, I think it must have been when the pregnant lady got dizzy. That incident drew everyone's attention, including Melvin's, and when he got distracted, I figure that's when Todd dropped the ring in his pocket."

"Yeah, the timing of her dizzy spell is definitely noteworthy."

"So do you think the pregnant lady was working with Todd?"

"Let's just say I'm considering it."

◆ ◆ ◆ ◆

A few seconds after Wes left the room, Shaheen reappeared and asked me to follow him to one of their VIP lounges where I could interview Melvin Williams in private.

As I followed him down the hallway, I said, "When I finish speaking with Melvin, I'll be heading over to DCSS headquarters, but I'll be back tomorrow morning to interview the rest of your employees."

"Any idea when that will be?"

"Unless I call and tell you otherwise, I'll plan to be here at ten-thirty in the morning. Once I've finished speaking with them, if my investigation doesn't lead me in another direction, I'll start concentrating on Todd Harriman."

"I can't imagine it leading you to anyone but Todd," Shaheen said, opening the door to one of their VIP lounges, "but I'll try to keep an open mind about it."

I had my doubts Shaheen would be able to do that, but naturally, I didn't voice those misgivings. Fortunately, I didn't have to say anything, because when we walked in the VIP lounge, Shaheen immediately started pointing out the different features of the room, something I felt sure he'd done many times before.

The room resembled the living area of a small luxury apartment, with a couch and chairs arranged around a rectangular glass-topped coffee table. There was also a beverage cart on one side of the room, and on the other side were several tall cabinets—much like china cabinets—with various pieces of jewelry on display.

None of the pieces had any prices on them.

"This is one of our hideaway lounges where our VIP customers are able to do their shopping in private. As you can see, there's comfortable seating, plenty of beverages, and with some advanced planning, we can also offer a catered meal."

"It looks very inviting."

Shaheen pointed over to the couch. "Have a seat. I'm sure Melvin will be here in a minute."

No sooner had he spoken than Melvin walked in the door.

I thought he seemed a little nervous as Shaheen was introducing us, but when his boss left and the two of us sat down together—he sat on the couch, and I sat across from him in a wingback chair—he appeared to be more at ease.

"I'm sure these last couple of days have been difficult for you," I said, trying to help him relax.

Melvin, who appeared to be in his late fifties and was dressed in a Gadise Diamonds black blazer with a white shirt and red tie, said, "Yes, they certainly have, but after going over what happened a hundred times, I can't think of anything I would have done differently."

"In a moment, I'll ask you to give me your perspective on how things played out, but first, I'd like to ask you a few questions."

"Sure. I'm happy to answer whatever questions you have for me."

"How well do you and Todd know each other?"

He stiffened a little. "Uh . . . I'm not sure I understand what you mean by 'know each other.' I know who Todd Harriman is, but I'm not friends with him, and I've never spoken to him except in a professional sense when he was in the showroom."

"That's basically what I'm asking you. When I was watching the video from the security cameras, I got the impression you recognized him, and from what I could tell, you seemed happy to see him."

He bobbed his head up and down a couple of times. "Well, of course I was. His father owns the Market Center. If there's anyone who could afford the jewelry in our store, it would be him. I was also glad I was the one who was available to help him."

"Okay, that makes sense. I also watched what was transpiring in the store before Todd came in, and I was wondering if you saw anything unusual or if anything got your attention."

Melvin looked down at his feet a moment as he thought about my question. "Hmmm. Let's see. I can't think of anything. We had just opened the doors, so we weren't very busy yet."

"Okay, so tell me what happened when you were helping Todd, and since I've already seen the video, I'd primarily like to know what you were thinking when you were showing him the signet rings."

Melvin sat back on the couch, rested his right elbow on one of the decorative throw pillows, and began his narrative. "When I greeted Todd and asked him how I could help him, he said he wanted to see some diamond signet rings. My immediate thought was that he had something definite in mind, and if I could figure out what he wanted, then I could probably make the sale."

"He didn't mention the price range?"

"No, but knowing his finances, I didn't think it mattered. When I brought out the smaller carat diamond rings, he didn't show much interest in them, and since he never tried them on, it didn't surprise me when he asked to see the ones with the larger carats."

"Was Todd saying anything to you as you were helping him? I really couldn't tell on the video."

"He occasionally said something about one of the rings, but he wasn't asking me for a description of them, and he didn't say anything of a personal nature to me."

"Did he seem nervous at all?"

"No, he didn't seem nervous, although he did look down at his watch several times."

"Like he was bored?"

"No, it was more like he had an appointment, and he was watching the time."

"Okay, so what happened when you brought out the larger carat diamond rings?"

"That's when his interest picked up. He tried on several rings, and at this point he started asking about prices. It was obvious the $65,000 ring piqued his interest the most. He tried it on, took it off, tried it on again, and looked at it from every angle. When I saw how much he liked it, I tried not to do too much of a sales job on him because I thought he was in the process of selling himself on the idea of buying it. I admit I stopped watching him at one point when I noticed one of our customers seemed to be in distress. That's when I—"

"—you mean the pregnant woman?"

"Yes, the pregnant woman. When I noticed Elizabeth was having her sit down, I wondered if we were about to have a baby born right here in the store. I was really afraid that was about to happen."

"You looked pretty worried in the video."

"I *was* worried, and that distracted me. The next thing I knew, Todd was shaking his head and saying he couldn't make up his mind. A few seconds later, he waved at me and left the store."

"Did his abruptness seem strange to you?"

Melvin adjusted the cuff on his white dress shirt and shook his head. "No, I wouldn't say it seemed strange. A lot of our customers, especially those who have more money than they know what to do with, frequently treat sales associates with a certain degree of rudeness. I was more concerned about the pregnant lady."

"But she was fine, wasn't she? I understand she just got dizzy."

"Yes, she left a few minutes after Todd did."

"So take me through what happened when you realized the $65,000 ring was missing."

He touched his hand to his forehead a moment. "Oh, that was awful. I didn't immediately realize it, though."

"Is that because you put away the least expensive rings first?"

"That's right. The larger carats go in a different display case, and when I looked at the tray where I'd placed them and saw there were only four rings, and I knew I'd brought out five, I really thought I was about to have a heart attack. Seriously, my heart was racing."

"I've been in some tough situations before so I know that feeling."

"It occurred to me Todd could have dropped it on the floor, although I didn't really believe that happened because I felt sure I would have noticed it. I still spent a few minutes looking for it, but when I didn't find it, I reported the missing ring to Wes, our security guard, and we both searched for it again. When we didn't find it, I had to go tell Phillip what happened."

"I'm sure that must have been hard."

"It was excruciating, but once I explained everything, he took it pretty well. He was adamant Todd stole the ring. He certainly didn't blame me for its disappearance."

"No, he views you as a man of integrity, and I commend you for that. Having a good reputation is worth more than a bucket full of diamonds."

Melvin smiled for the first time. "Well, thank you, Mr. McKay, but I can't take credit for my honesty. I'm a Christian, and I try to live a life that's pleasing to Jesus Christ. He's always with me, and whenever I'm tempted to stray from his commands, I try to remember that. I don't mean to sound preachy, and I hope you're not offended."

"No, I'm not offended. I actually appreciate what you said. I'm also a Christian, so I can identify with what you're saying."

"Yes, I thought so. I admit I was nervous about talking to you, but you've made it easy on me. I haven't felt like you were judging me for being careless either. Phillip told me you're the head of a security firm, but as I've thought about it, I really believe I followed all the security protocols."

"It appears that way from viewing the videos, and I certainly don't fault you for showing concern for the woman who looked like she was about to have a baby. I'm surprised she was here looking at diamond bracelets in the first place."

"I'm just thankful she was all right."

"I'm curious if she was a regular customer or if you remember seeing her in the store before."

"No, she's not one of our regular customers. I have a good memory for faces, and I've never seen her in Gadise Diamonds before."

"Okay. Well thanks, Melvin. You've given me some useful information."

"I'm not sure how you'll be able to prove Todd took the ring. That seems like an impossible task to me."

"It may seem that way at the moment, but you'd be surprised at how often an insignificant detail can blow a case wide open."

"Well, I certainly hope that happens this time."

"So do I."

If it didn't, I wasn't optimistic this case would end satisfactorily for anyone, except maybe Todd Harriman.

### End of Chapter Four

To continue reading *Two Believe*, you can visit the author's website, **www.LuanaEhrlich.com** and click on the link to purchase the book through Amazon or go directly to the Amazon website and enter the name of the book followed by the author's name.

Luana loves to hear from her readers. Contact her through her email: **author@luanaehrlich.com**.

# List of Books
## by Luana Ehrlich

Each book can be read as a standalone novel, but for readers who prefer a series experience, the following order is suggested.

### The Titus Ray Thriller Series:

*One Step Back*, the prequel to *One Night in Tehran*

*One Night in Tehran*, Book I

*Two Days in Caracas*, Book II

*Three Weeks in Washington*, Book III

*Four Months in Cuba,* Book IV

*Five Years in Yemen*, Book V

*Two Steps Forward,* Book VI

*Three Steps Away*, Book VII

*Four Steps Missed*, Book VIII

*Five Steps Beyond*, Book IX (Coming in 2023)

### The Mylas Grey Mystery Series:

*One Day Gone*, Book I

*Two Days Taken*, Book II

*Three Days Clueless,* Book III

*Four Days Famous*, Book IV

*Five Days Lost*, Book V

### The Ben Mitchell/Titus Ray Thriller Series:

*Ben in Love,* Book I

*Ben in Charge*, Book II

*Ben in Trouble*, Book III

### The Silas McKay Suspense Series:

*One Wonders*, Book I

*Two Believe,* Book II

*Three Confess,* Book III (coming in 2023)

Made in the USA
Columbia, SC
24 January 2025

52516192R00098